"Captivating . . . A deliciously duplicitous psychological thriller that will lure readers until the wee hours and beyond. With a plot equally as twisty, spellbinding, and addictive as Gillian Flynn's *Gone Girl* or Paula Hawkins's *The Girl on the Train*, this is sure to be a hit with suspense fans." —*Library Journal*, starred review

"Constantine's debut novel is the work of two sisters in collaboration, and these ladies definitely know the formula. A *Gone Girl*–esque confection with villainy and melodrama galore." —*Kirkus Reviews*, starred review

"To the pantheon of *Gone Girl*–type bad girls you can now add Amber Patterson, the heroine of this devilishly ingenious debut thriller. . . . The reader watches with shock and delight as Amber cold-bloodedly manipulates Daphne and Jackson and lays waste to anyone else who stands in her way. . . . To say any more would spoil all the twists that Constantine (the pseudonym of sisters Lynne and Valerie Constantine) has in store along the way to a surprising and entirely satisfying ending. Suffice it to say that readers would have to go back to the likes of Ira Levin's *A Kiss Before Dying* or Patricia Highsmith's *The Talented Mr. Ripley* to find as entertaining a depiction of a sociopathic monster." —*Publishers Weekly*, starred review

"The twists keep coming in this psychological roller coaster from debut author Constantine, the pen name of sisters Lynne and Valerie Constantine . . . This is a satisfying thriller that offers a window into the darker side of glamorous lives and powerful men." —*Booklist*

"Wonderfully plausible, hypnotically compelling, and deliciously chilling and creepy—some of the best psychological suspense you'll read this year." —Lee Child,
#1 *New York Times*–bestselling author of the Jack Reacher Novels

"A wonderfully clever story, filled with suspense and a shocking twist."
—Jane Green, *New York Times*–bestselling author of *The Sunshine Sisters*

"An extraordinary debut and gripping psychological thriller that is full of unexpected twists. Readers will become obsessed with these chilling characters who pull you in and refuse to let go."
—Sara Blaedel,
Denmark's international-bestselling "Queen of Crime"

"A beautifully constructed set piece, an intricate narrative that doubles back and folds in on itself like a Mobius strip, revealing secret upon secret, and layer upon layer, with a seductive 'just one more chapter' urgency that will keep readers up all night. Giving new meaning to the adage 'be careful what you wish for,' *The Last Mrs. Parrish* proves that the worst that can happen just might be when you get what you want. Addictive!"
—Karen Dionne,
author of *The Marsh King's Daughter*

"Gillian Flynn meets Joy Fielding . . . In an age of great anti-heroines, comes the most unlikeable one yet, the coldly devilish Amber Patterson. This thriller delivers the most satisfying ending since B.A. Paris' smash hit *Behind Closed Doors*—and a victorious romp of revenge." —Jenny Milchman, *USA Today*–bestselling author of *Cover of Snow, Ruin Falls*

The Next Mrs. Parrish

"The perfect summer beach read." —Katie Couric Media

"Delicious and shocking, *The Next Mrs. Parrish* is an incredibly entertaining and compulsive tale of revenge and deception you won't want to miss." —Jeneva Rose, *New York Times*–bestselling author of *You Shouldn't Have Come Here*

"A brilliant page-turner where nothing (and no one) is what it seems . . . Pour a glass of wine and settle in for the ride." —Lisa Gardner, #1 *New York Times*–bestselling author of *Before She Disappeared*

"Sizzles with devious characters, head-spinning twists, and a breathless game of cat and mouse. Constantine fans are in for a treat—and one hell of a ride!"   —Andrea Bartz,
New York Times–bestselling author of The Spare Room

"The players are about to get played. You'll devour this juicy, twisty psychological thriller in one sitting!"   —Lisa Scottoline,
#1 bestselling author of The Truth About the Devlins

"Get ready for a roller coaster of suspense. . . . Delightful and addictive, I loved this riveting read!"   —Jean Kwok,
New York Times–bestselling author of Girl in Translation

"To die for!"   —Vanessa Lillie, USA Today–bestselling author
of Blood Sisters

"Masterful. Enthralling. Diabolical."   —Michele Campbell,
international-bestselling author of The Intern

"Fans of the first book will eat this up."   —Publishers Weekly

"With scheming worthy of the soapiest television drama, readers will enjoy watching the match of wits and wills in this entertaining beach read."   —Library Journal

"The timeless battle between good and evil has never been trashier. Hooray."   —Kirkus Reviews

The Senator's Wife

"Backstabbing, gaslighting, and double-crossing—The Senator's Wife has all you want in a thriller and all that you fear to be true about Washington."   —The Washington Post

"Anyone who still misses watching Kerry Washington in *Scandal* won't want to miss Constantine's *The Senator's Wife*, a delicious concoction of political intrigue, medical mystery, and psychological suspense. . . . Be prepared: You'll be tempted to finish this one in a single sitting." —*Parade*

"A deadly cocktail of medical mystery, family drama, and psychological suspense—I'll admit, *The Senator's Wife* really got me."
—Chandler Baker, *New York Times*–bestselling author of *Whisper Network*

"A high-stakes paranoia thriller, slippery as a politician's handshake, that's both sophisticated and irrepressibly fun." —A. J. Finn, #1 *New York Times*–bestselling author of *The Woman in the Window*

"A scandalous tale by the master of suspense. I was unable to put it down until I knew how it was going to end—because I couldn't possibly have guessed." —Sandie Jones, *New York Times*–bestselling author of *The Other Woman*

"A thrilling new story from Liv Constantine set in the dark heart of Washington, DC, *The Senator's Wife* is full of grit, grift, and tons of insider secrets. It's insidiously clever and utterly mesmerizing."
—J. T. Ellison, *New York Times*–bestselling author of *It's One of Us*

"Another twisty triumph for bestseller Liv Constantine. I devoured this thoroughly entertaining, well-crafted thriller. If you loved *The Last Mrs. Parrish*, you'll want to pick up this book."
—Sarah Pekkanen, *New York Times*–bestselling author of *Gone Tonight*

"A high-stakes, propulsive thriller that leaves readers breathless as the characters' colliding secrets and agendas unfold." —Nina Sadowsky, author of *Privacy* and *The Burial Society*

MY SISTER'S DAUGHTER

AND

SILENT ECHO

MY SISTER'S DAUGHTER

DAUGHTER

AND

SILENT ECHO

TWO THRILLERS

LIV CONSTANTINE

Podium

Copyright © 2025 by Lynne Constantine

Cover design by James Iacobelli

ISBN: 978-1-0394-7971-5

Published in 2025 by Podium Publishing
www.podiumentertainment.com

Podium

CONTENTS

MY SISTER'S DAUGHTER

AND

SILENT ECHO

MY
SISTER'S
DAUGHTER

To my sweet nieces, Valerie, Samantha, and Alexa,
whose motives I've never had to question. xo

CHAPTER ONE

It's the life-changing events that you never see coming.

I almost don't answer my phone. All morning there have been nonstop interruptions, and I need to finish editing the images for the author I photographed last week. I sigh as I walk over to the kitchen counter where my phone sits and glance at the screen. I'm about to let it go to voicemail when I notice the 267 area code. I swipe.

"Hello?"

A male voice I don't recognize speaks. "Is this Ashley Bowers?"

"Yes, who's calling?"

"Detective Minsk from the Bucks County Sheriff department. I'm afraid I have some bad news."

I grip the phone tighter. "What is it?"

"I'm sorry to tell you that your sister Courtney drowned last night. As you're her only next of kin besides her teenage daughter, we need you to come as soon as possible to make arrangements for her."

I sink down into the kitchen chair, shock leaving me momentarily speechless. Courtney is dead?

"What happened?"

"Her daughter called 911 this morning when she found her in the pool."

I gasp. "Oh my God!"

"We're still investigating, but as of now it looks like an accidental drowning."

"Of course. I'll leave right away." I grab a pen, scribble down the detective's contact number, and end the call. Visions of my sister floating in the pool come unbidden. I push them from my mind as I start to clear my schedule. Courtney's daughter, Serena, is only thirteen years old. The poor child, finding her mother like that. And less than a year after losing her father in that terrible freak accident.

I've never met my niece, only seen pictures from stealing looks on Facebook and Instagram. Courtney and I haven't spoken in over thirteen years. Now we never will. Our relationship had always been complicated. Sometimes I wonder if, when there are only two of you, your roles are cast early on. As the firstborn, I was a rule follower, studious, and I basked in my parents' approval. Courtney, born two years later, was rebellious, stubborn, and determined to do things her way. Stunningly beautiful, with delicate features, cornflower-blue eyes, and white-blond hair, she looked like an angel. But her nature was volatile. My earliest childhood memories are of slamming doors, threats of time-outs, and unfavorable comparisons where my parents often shouted at Courtney: *Why can't you be more like your sister?*

I'd try to give her advice on how to get along better with our parents, but they never really understood her, and she felt it. As she got older, she'd have fits of rage where she would punch holes in the walls and break things. I was usually the only one who could calm her, but there were times she even took her anger out on me. The rift between her and my parents grew as she did, but when I was around to play peacemaker things weren't too bad. Then I moved to Boston for college, and she felt abandoned. She started drinking, breaking curfew, and letting her grades go to hell. She managed to graduate, but decided college wasn't for her and got a job working at an art gallery. I thought it was a perfect fit for her. She was struggling to stay sober, and over the next several years, was in and out of rehab at my parents' expense. The only reason she kept her job throughout it all was because the owner of the gallery was a recovering alcoholic and cut her a lot of slack.

When I came back to Baltimore after college, things had changed between us. I don't think she ever really forgave me for going so far away and leaving her alone. She began to resent me, and the bond we'd shared before slowly disintegrated.

I had thought that one day, Courtney and I would find our way back to each other. I wipe a tear from my cheek. That will never happen now. But I'll take care of her daughter. Maybe this will be a second chance for me—an opportunity to make it up to my sister somehow. Courtney's husband, Bobby's, parents are gone, and he had no siblings. I'm Serena's only living relative now. Serena needs me. And I need her too.

Sherlock, our Bernese Mountain Dog, pads up to me and puts his head on my knee.

"You can always tell when someone's sad," I say, ruffling his fur. He sits down, his head now on my foot, and continues to stare at me. The sound of the door opening rouses him, and he runs toward it. Elliott's home with the kids. I blow out a breath and check my reflection in the microwave. I don't want the kids to see that I've been crying.

"Mommy, Mommy, look what I made!"

Maddox, our four-year-old, bursts into the kitchen holding a painting on canvas. "A T-rex!" Bright green paint covers most of the space and the likeness is decent. He beams as he holds it out for me to look at.

"Wow, amazing! Where should we put it?"

"My room."

Elliott and our twelve-year-old, Luna, come in behind him.

"I'm starving, what's there to eat?" my daughter asks.

"Um, I made some cookies this morning. Can you give Maddox some too? I need to talk to Dad upstairs for a minute."

She shrugs and pulls out two plates. "Okay."

Elliott gives me a concerned look but says nothing.

"Let's go upstairs a minute."

When we reach our bedroom, I shut the door. "I got some bad news today."

"What is it?"

"Courtney. She . . ." I burst into tears before I can finish the sentence.

Elliott pulls me into him for a hug. "What's going on?"

"She's dead," I manage to get out in between sobs.

"What? How?"

I compose myself and fill him in.

"I'm so sorry. When are you leaving?"

"Now. I don't want to bring the kids. Can you work from home for the next couple of days? I've already canceled all my photo sessions for the next two weeks."

He nods. "Of course. I don't have any client meetings this week so it's no problem. I'm so sorry, Ash. This is unbelievable. But are you sure you don't want me to come with you? We could get a sitter for the kids."

I shake my head. "I don't want to overwhelm Serena, and I don't know how long I'll need to be there. I texted Marilyn to let her know and she said to tell you that she and Henry can help out if you need anything." Marilyn is a good friend who lives a few houses up the road. She has a daughter, Willow, who's Luna's age, and a son, Simon, Maddox's age.

"I should be able to be here, but good to know."

"Listen, you need to prepare the kids for Serena coming back with me."

He gives me a confused look. "What do you mean?"

"She's going to live with us, of course. She doesn't have anyone else."

His eyes widen. "Um, don't you think we should at least discuss this? She's, what, thirteen, and we've never even met her?"

My mouth drops open. "Are you serious? How can you think this is up for debate? I'm not going to put my niece in foster care. It's not her fault we haven't met her. I won't hold her responsible for my sister's behavior."

"You're right, of course, it's just, from what you've told me about your childhood, Courtney was a lot. I worry about our kids. What if the apple didn't fall far from the tree? Serena and Luna will be in the same grade at school. I don't want her to be a bad influence on our daughter."

I shake my head, too overwhelmed to consider what he's saying. "First things first. We'll figure it out, okay? She's family. That's all that matters."

CHAPTER
TWO

I drive two and a half hours to my sister's house, where a social worker is waiting with my niece. I park the car in front of a formal-looking stone colonial on a beautifully landscaped half acre in a neighborhood where it's obvious the homeowners take great care in maintaining their property. It's so much more buttoned-up than my sister ever was, but I suppose she adapted to a different lifestyle. I feel nervous when I ring the bell. Surely Serena will wonder where I've been all her life. I have no idea what Courtney has told her. It shouldn't be this way—me waiting for a stranger to open the door to my sister's house. I feel ill prepared to be confronted with the remnants of her life. I breathe deeply and the door is opened by a young woman in a gray suit.

"Mrs. Bowers?" she asks, and I nod.

She extends her hand. "Becky Marshall."

I enter the house and take in the traditional style. Clean lines, monochrome color scheme. It's a bit sterile, so unlike the Courtney I remember. I try to imagine her life here but I come up short. The truth is that I don't know anything about her anymore.

"Serena's in her room packing her things. Shall I take you up?"

Swallowing the lump in my throat, I follow her up the stairs. I hold my breath as she turns the knob on the door, then release it in a whoosh when I see the young girl standing there. She's the spitting image of my sister. It's as though I'm looking at a young Courtney. Serena looks up and our eyes meet, and it takes everything I have not to rush in and envelop her in a hug. I hold back a sob as the realization that I'll never see my sister again hits me with gale force. She's really gone. Courtney's dead. I struggle to keep my composure.

"Hi, Serena. I'm your aunt Ashley."

A beat before she answers. Then, in clipped tones, "Yeah. I know."

"I'm so sorry about your mom. I can't even imagine what you're going through."

She doesn't respond, merely stares at me.

I clear my throat. "Well, I suppose you've been told that you'll be coming home with me. I hope that's okay with you."

"Like I have a choice?"

The social worker finally speaks. "Why don't I wait for you downstairs? Let you two get acquainted."

I walk over to the bed and sit on the edge. "I know this has got to be so hard for you. I hope you know that I loved your mom very much. I didn't want things to be . . ."

"I don't wanna talk about my mom."

"Okay. Can I help you?"

She shrugs and points to a stack of cardboard boxes on the floor. "You can put those together."

I get up and start assembling the boxes, glancing around her bedroom as I do so. Her room looks like a typical teen's. Purple walls, posters of bands, a corkboard with various stickers and notes. My eyes rest on a big red metal sign with a circle and a large A through it and the word "Anarchy" underneath it. A feeling of disquiet comes over me, and I think of Elliott's concerns. I hope that Serena hasn't inherited her mother's disposition along with her looks. When I've put all the boxes together, I turn to her.

"Would you like me to pack up the closet?"

"I'm good. Can you wait for me downstairs?"

"All right." I leave, shut the door behind me, and join Becky in the kitchen.

"She wanted to be alone," I say, feeling embarrassed for some reason.

"This has been extremely hard on her. It hasn't been that long since her father died. And never having met you . . ."

"I tried to be in my sister's life. She cut me off." I throw my hands up. "I guess it doesn't matter now. I'm going to do everything I can to make Serena feel welcome in her new home. My daughter's only a few months younger than Serena. I'm hoping she'll be able to make Serena feel more comfortable."

Becky nods. "It's great that she'll have a cousin so close to her age. But don't be surprised if it takes Serena a while to adjust. She's bound to feel resentful and angry. She was still mourning her father and now, this. As I told you on the phone, it's imperative that you avail yourselves of counseling services for the whole family. She and her mother were seeing a grief therapist here for a little while after Serena's father passed away. From what I've been told, the guidance counselor at her school has had a few sessions with Serena as well. Now that she's lost her mother, I strongly encourage you to all go to counseling together. I've already been in contact with the appropriate office in your state."

"Of course," I answer, but I'm not at all confident that Elliott will agree to it. He's not a fan of strangers digging into his personal business. "What's going to happen to the house?"

"It's being foreclosed by the bank. The sale is next week; all the contents have been seized as well. Serena's able to take only her clothing and personal belongings."

I shake my head. I don't understand how Courtney lost the house. "Did she stop making payments after Bobby died? What happened to his practice?" As far as I knew, her husband was a successful veterinarian. How did they get so behind on mortgage payments?

She hands me a piece of paper with a name and phone number. "Give their lawyer a call. He can share the details." She stands. "I'll mail you the documentation we discussed, but you're free to take Serena home when she's finished packing."

I thank her, and she leaves. I move over to the sliding glass door and look out at the pool. I can't bring myself to go outside, to stand in the place where my sister died. I shiver and close the blinds. Two hours later, we've loaded up the car and are ready to leave. I turn to my niece.

"I know you must have loved it here. It must be very hard having to leave it."

She looks down at the floor. "My mom said we lost the house because you stole her money."

CHAPTER
THREE

Serena was quiet for the entire car ride. When I tried to respond to her accusation, she put her hand up and told me she didn't want to talk about it. It's late by the time we get back to my house, and I'm hoping both kids are sleeping. I'd like to give Serena a chance to get settled in before meeting everyone. As we pull into the driveway, she looks around. "It's so deserted. Is there even a mall around here?"

Privacy is one of the things that attracted Elliott and me to our home in White Hall, Maryland, where our closest neighbor is a few miles away. It's peaceful and beautiful, but I can see how it would seem isolated to someone used to a neighborhood.

"There's a country store twenty minutes up the road, but the mall's about forty-five minutes away."

"Great," she mumbles under her breath.

I put the car in park and turn to her before opening the door. "How about if we just bring your suitcase in tonight and get the boxes tomorrow?"

"Whatever."

The house is lit by only a lamp in the hallway. "Your room's this way."

She follows me without a word, and I open the door to what has been, until now, a guest suite. It's on the third floor and has its own bathroom. Luna was hoping to move into it in a couple months on her thirteenth birthday, but naturally that won't happen now. "We'll redecorate it however you like."

"Okay."

"You have your own bathroom. I'll get you some towels. Do you need anything else?"

She shakes her head.

I lean in to give her a hug, and she stiffens. I pat her shoulder awkwardly. "Okay then, I'm just downstairs if you need anything."

I head to our bedroom. Elliott's awake and reading.

"Well?"

I shrug. "She's distant and grieving." I fill him in on the past several hours. "Courtney hasn't painted me in the best light. She told Serena they were losing the house because we stole her money."

"I can only imagine the narrative she's woven for that girl. Courtney always blamed everyone else for her mistakes." Elliott shakes his head.

He's not wrong, but as Courtney got older, she became more settled, and softer. When she met Bobby, it was a turning point for her. They got married when she was twenty-four. I was also engaged, and Elliott and I got married six months later. At that time, we were both in the same stage of life. We'd talk every day, help each other navigate the ups and downs of new marriages. Elliott and Bobby, while very different, got along well enough and the four of us spent a lot of our free time together. The distance between us vanished. Then everything went to hell when our parents died.

I think back to the last time I saw my sister. It was right after our parents' funeral. They'd died in a helicopter accident, and despite the heartbreak of losing them both at the same time, I knew that neither would have survived without the other. Our parents had always been inordinately close, almost to the exclusion of Courtney and me. They'd both loved adventure and shared all the same hobbies and interests. Once my sister and I were both out of high school, our parents were gone almost every other month, traveling the world. Our father's real estate investments over the years provided enough income for him to retire early and enjoy life.

Courtney and I held tightly to each other as we attended to all the details of their funerals. But when our family attorney read the will, everything changed. I'll never forget the look of pain on Courtney's face when he read our parents' last words to Courtney. *It is not an oversight that Courtney inherits nothing from us. We have already given her too much.* They left their house, as well as the lake house at Deep Creek Lake, to me. Up until that moment, I hadn't thought my parents were cruel. I reached a hand out to grab hers.

"I'm sorry, Court. That was wrong of them. I'll split everything with you. I'll sell their house and put your name on the deed to the Deep Creek house."

She snatched her hand back, a look of pure hatred in her eyes. "I should have known you couldn't be trusted. You're the executor, you had to know what the will said."

"No, I swear. I had no idea. I don't want this."

"I could never measure up to you. Admit it, you loved being the favorite. Mommy and Daddy's good little girl. I don't want anything from them. Or from you. There was never room for me in this family, and this just proves it. We're done." She jumped up from the chair and ran from the room.

I ran after her. "Wait, please. Don't blame this on me."

Courtney stopped and spun around. "If you hadn't always kissed their asses, being so perfect, they might have actually seen me." She was yelling. I tried to speak, but her tirade continued and drowned out my words. "You have no idea what it's been like living in your shadow my whole life. If you had stepped out of line once in a while, they would have gone easier on me. Enjoy your blood money."

Shortly afterward, she and Bobby moved to Pennsylvania. I tried to give her half of the money. I sent a check, which was returned, cut in pieces. I even went to Bobby, pleading with him to accept the money, but he didn't want to go against Courtney's wishes. I knew they could use the money. Bobby still had major debt from vet school. Our parents' estate had been worth over three million dollars. But no matter how hard I tried, Courtney refused it. She always did cut off her nose to spite her face. After that, she made it clear that she wanted nothing to do with me, that I was dead to her, and after months and months of pursuing her, I finally stopped trying. When I heard that she'd had a daughter, Elliott reached out to Bobby and he agreed to allow us to put one and a half million dollars in a trust for Serena without letting Courtney know. When I had Luna, I tried again, thinking motherhood might bond us, but she still wouldn't speak to me.

I turn to Elliott. "After Bobby died, she would have been informed about the trust. What the hell happened to that money?"

"What did their lawyer say?"

"I haven't reached him yet. Hopefully he'll call me back tomorrow."

"Any new information on how Courtney drowned?"

"They'll know more after the autopsy. But it looks like she fell and hit her head. Apparently, there was an empty bottle of wine and a broken glass on the deck." I shake my head. "I guess she started drinking again."

"That's awful. And Serena found her the next morning?"

"Yeah. She woke up and went looking for her. Found her in the pool." I shudder. "I can't even imagine it."

"Well, let's try and get some sleep." He closes his eyes.

I turn the light off and settle under the covers, exhausted from the day. Just as I begin to doze off, a bloodcurdling scream pierces the silence.

CHAPTER
FOUR

Elliott and I jump out of bed and run from the room. Another scream rings out, and I realize it's coming from upstairs. I rush into the bedroom to see Serena thrashing in bed, yelling out. I gently grab her shoulders, trying to wake her.

"Serena, Serena, wake up, honey."

She lets out another moan and slowly her eyes focus on me. She throws her arms around my neck, clinging to me as she sobs. "I can't stop seeing her."

I hold her. "Shh, it's okay. It's going to be okay."

"I'm scared, Aunt Ashley," she whispers, and for the first time today I feel her tough exterior crumbling to show the young girl underneath. Of course she's scared. Her whole world has fallen apart.

"I'm here, sweetie."

"What's going on?" Luna walks in the room, rubbing her eyes. She looks from me to Serena and then back again. "Is this her?"

This is not the way I wanted them to meet. "Luna, this is your cousin Serena. She had a nightmare. It's late, go back to bed. We'll talk more tomorrow."

"Hi, Serena. I'm sorry about your mom," Luna says.

Serena doesn't answer her and clings to me more tightly. "Can you stay with me, Aunt Ashley?"

"Of course."

Elliott ushers Luna from the room, and I tuck Serena back in. I move over to the loveseat by the window. "I'll sleep here tonight."

She closes her eyes and whispers a thank-you. The pull of sleep is irresistible and seconds later I give in to it.

I wake up at dawn to find Serena sound asleep. I slip from the room and go downstairs.

The house is quiet, everyone still in bed. I've been so focused on the logistics of getting Serena here that I've barely had time to grieve my sister. Not a day has gone by that I haven't thought about her. I can't count the number of times I've picked up the phone, ready to call her, and then changed my mind. I'll regret that for the rest of my life. But for now, there are lists to be made, conversations to be had, and errands to run. I'm grateful that it's Saturday and our schedule is clear for the day.

"Mom?"

I turn to see Luna walking toward me, still half asleep, one fist rubbing an eye.

"You're up early. Come sit," I say, patting the cushion next to me.

She plops down next to me. "Why'd you give Serena the loft room? You promised I could have it."

I sigh. "Sweetie, I'm sorry, but it was the only empty room. I didn't think you'd want to share a room with your cousin since you've never met her."

She rolls her eyes. "Why can't she have my room, and I move into the loft now?"

I'm still so exhausted that I can barely think straight. I shrug. "Her coming here was all so sudden, and I didn't want her to feel like she was intruding, so I wanted to give her her own room right away. And I just think it's better for her to have a little extra space. Try to understand."

"Like, I'm sorry about what happened to her and all, but it's not fair. I've been looking forward to having it. Now she gets it?"

I shift so that I'm facing her and put a hand on her shoulder. "Honey, I understand that you're disappointed, and I don't blame you. But you have to think about everything Serena's been through. In the past year, she's lost both of her parents. She's had to come and live in a strange house with people she's never met. To leave her school and all her friends. Can you imagine how devastated you would be? I really need you to try to support her. She's your cousin. I bet in no time the two of you will be best friends."

She gives me a dubious look, but slowly nods. "Yeah, okay. I'll try. But it's weird. Having a stranger live here."

"She's not a stranger. She's family." I stand. "Hungry? I was going to make pancakes."

She doesn't respond, and I go back to the kitchen. Minutes later, Maddox comes crashing in with Elliott behind him.

"Mommy, Mommy. Can we go jump?"

I pick him up and give him a kiss. Maddox's preschool teacher suggested we buy an indoor trampoline to help him expend some energy. He's been a whirling dervish from the time he was born and needs lots of physical activity to help center him. Elliott surprised everyone with a full-size outdoor trampoline with a netting enclosure, and it's all Maddox wants to do now.

"After breakfast." I put him down, and he runs over to his sister, jumping on the cushion next to her.

"Watch it!" she scolds as he falls into her.

"Can we get my stuff from the car?"

I look up to see Serena. I didn't hear her come in.

"Morning, Serena. Of course. Just let me finish with these pancakes."

She stands there looking uncomfortable.

"Do you want something to drink, sweetie?"

She shakes her head. "Can I just have the car keys? I can get my stuff."

Luna comes over. "I'll help you, Serena."

I smile, grateful at Luna's sudden thoughtfulness. I was prepared for some jealousy on Luna's part—sharing is sometimes difficult for her. Maybe things are going to turn out better than I'd thought.

* * *

After Serena's belongings are all moved in, she and I make a plan to go to the mall to pick up some things to make the room hers. Elliott and Maddox have taken Luna to her soccer practice. I'm making a list while I wait for Serena to come downstairs when my phone rings.

"Hello?"

"Mrs. Bowers?"

"This is she."

"This is Noel Sinclair, your sister's attorney. I understand you have some questions about the estate."

"Yes. I'm trying to understand how the house fell into foreclosure. We set up a trust for Serena years ago for one and a half million dollars, and it should be worth even more now. Why wasn't that used to pay the mortgage if Courtney was falling behind after Bobby's death?"

He clears his throat. "Bobby must have gone through it before he died. He had liquidated all their assets."

"I don't understand. He spent all the money?"

"Bobby had a gambling problem. He came to me a few weeks before his accident. He was ready to declare bankruptcy. He'd borrowed against his vet practice and lost that money, and then he went through the rest of their assets."

I can't believe this. "Did Courtney know?"

"He kept it from her, but by the time he came clean with me, he had to tell her too. He couldn't hide it anymore."

"And when he died, no insurance?"

"He had whole life and . . ."

"Let me guess, he borrowed against that too. So, he left her with nothing but debt."

"I'm afraid so."

"I wish she would have told me." A thought occurs to me. "My sister's drowning. Are the police sure that it wasn't intentional? Is there any chance she . . ."

"There's been no indication of suicide, if that's what you're asking, but you'd need to speak to the police for more information."

"Thank you."

"Of course. Please let me know if there's anything else I can do."

I end the call, my thoughts racing. How long had Bobby had a gambling addiction? And what other secrets have yet to surface?

CHAPTER
FIVE

It's been two weeks since Serena came to live with us, and things are beginning to settle down. While Luna and Serena haven't really bonded, they're civil to each other, and Serena has taken a strong liking to Maddox. Luna and her brother spend more time bickering than playing, so it's a real blessing to have someone help out with Maddox. She builds Legos with him, takes him out on the trampoline, and is even helping him learn how to draw. I had no idea she was an artist, but she's quite good, and when she's drawing in her sketch pad, she seems almost happy. Courtney was a good artist too.

"When's Serena coming home?" Maddox asks, looking up from his Erector Set. Elliott and I always joke that he's our little engineer. He loves taking things apart and putting them back together again. The set he's working on now is a car model for kids eight to twelve, but the sets for his own age bore him.

I glance at my watch. "Soon, buddy. Do you want to rest for a bit?" He's home from preschool today with a low-grade fever.

He shakes his head, still concentrating on his build. The sound of the front door chime makes me look up, and Luna and Serena rush in.

"Moooom," Luna calls out as she runs toward me.

"Hi, girls."

Luna stops in my direction with Serena close behind. "Coach hardly let me play today," she says, casting a derisive look at Serena. "Why does she have to play goalie too?"

"It's not my fault that I'm better than you," Serena says, her face red.

"I wish you'd never come here," Luna yells and runs from the room.

I walk over to Serena and put an arm around her. "I'm sorry. She didn't mean that."

Maddox runs to her and grabs her hand. "Come see my car."

She allows him to pull her over to where he was building.

"I'll be right back," I tell them. Luna's door is shut and when I turn the handle, I realize she's locked it. I bang on the door. "Open the door this instant."

It swings open, and I enter. She sits on the bed, her arms crossed, then wipes a tear from her cheek. "It's not fair."

I shut the door and sit next to her. "Luna, what you said was very hurtful. I won't have it."

"I mean it. Why did she have to come? All my friends think she's so cool, and it's like she's trying to take over my life. And now she's on the soccer team, and Coach likes her better than me."

I put my arm around her. "I doubt he likes her better, honey. Maybe he's just trying to make her feel at home. I know this is hard, but you have to realize it's even harder for Serena. I know you can find it in your heart to be more patient and welcoming to your cousin."

She shakes her head. "I'm trying, but she doesn't want to be friends with me. She's only nice to everyone else. And she acts like Maddox is *her* brother."

I don't remind her that she doesn't exactly make time for Maddox. "Serena is doing her best to fit in. Try to imagine if you were in her shoes. If you had to go live with her family."

She rolls her eyes. "Yeah, yeah. I know."

"You can start by apologizing to her." I stand and hold out my hand to her. She takes it, and we go back to the kitchen together.

"I'm sorry, Serena. I didn't mean it." Her apology is perfunctory at best.

Serena looks up and smiles sweetly. "It's okay, Luna. Want to play a game?"

"I have homework," she says.

Serena shrugs. "Okay." She looks up again. "I like your necklace."

Luna's hand goes to the gold chain with a round gold and silver compass charm. "It belonged to my mom's mom, my grandmother."

Serena arches an eyebrow. "My grandmother too."

Luna stares at her. "Yeah, I guess so. I never got to meet her, but she wanted me to have it. My mom said it's always been handed down to the first granddaughter."

"Okay, why don't you go ahead and get started on that homework," I say. Luna crosses her arms, not moving. Serena turns her attention back to Maddox, and I breathe a sigh of relief. Sherlock is sitting at her feet and Serena rubs his head.

"I always wanted a dog."

"Well, now you have one," I say.

"Sherlock is mine," Luna says. "I'm the one who named him."

Serena doesn't look at her but continues to pet him. "You don't give him much attention."

Luna shakes her head. "Come on, Sherlock," she calls. He doesn't move. Serena's mouth curves into a small smile.

"Sherlock!" Luna tries again, but he stays put.

"Oh whatever!" she says as she stomps away.

Later, after everyone's in bed, Elliott and I sit by the fire with glasses of wine. "It's so nice to have some peace and quiet," I say, taking a sip of my cabernet.

"Luna told me about the soccer team. It's a good thing you at least made sure they're not in the same class."

I nod. "Yeah, I didn't think about the downside of their being so similar in age. Something really awkward happened today too."

"What?"

I tell him about my mother's necklace. "As soon as the words left

Luna's lips about it going to the oldest granddaughter, I realized it should be Serena's. She was born first."

Elliott puts his glass down and gives me a long look. "That must have been very awkward, but you're not thinking of taking it from Luna, are you?"

"Of course not. I'm just saying, it's another reminder of my parents' favoritism. My mother gave that to me right after we were married. She had no idea whether the first granddaughter would come from Courtney or me. But she sidelined Courtney again."

He sighs and takes my hand in his. "I'm so sorry this is bringing all of that up for you. Remember, though, you're not your mother and you can't take responsibility for her mistakes. Things will work out, we just need to give it some time."

He leans in and kisses me, and I lean into him. His hand moves to my breast and I feel the stirring of desire. "Let's go upstairs," he whispers, his voice husky.

I follow wordlessly, eager to forget my troubles in his embrace, if only for a little while. He locks the door behind us, then we put our wine down and fall into bed. He runs his hands all over me and for the first time in weeks, I let myself relax and forget about everything but him.

CHAPTER
SIX

Elliott's been in Orlando for three days for a client meeting/golf tournament with his high-net-worth wealth management clients. I can't wait for him to return tomorrow. His steadying presence is the only thing keeping me centered right now. My desire to help Serena and my concern over how this is affecting Luna is pulling me in two. Serena's soccer skills are far superior to Luna's, and Luna keeps complaining about it. I love my daughter, but I'm aware of her shortcomings. She can be a sore loser. I made an appointment with the family therapist that the social worker recommended and, to my surprise, Elliott agreed to go.

Maddox and Serena are outside on the trampoline and I smile watching their happy faces, their laughter lifting my spirits. Loud footsteps on the stairs get my attention. Luna comes running into the kitchen.

"Look what she did!" she yells, holding out a pink sweater.

"What are you talking about?"

Her face is red. "She ruined it!"

The material is shredded with long cuts all along the front. I take it from her, examining it.

"This is . . . I don't understand."

"She did it. She knows it's my favorite sweater and she cut it up to spite me. I hate her!"

"Calm down. I'm sure there's a reasonable explanation. You can't just accuse Serena of this."

She scoffs. "Are you totally clueless? Who else would do it?" Before I can stop her, she runs outside toward the trampoline. I follow quickly.

"Luna, stop!" I call, but she ignores me. Maddox and Serena stop jumping as Luna stands at the opening.

"Why did you do this?"

Serena climbs out and Maddox follows behind her.

"Do what?"

"You cut my sweater up."

Serena's expression is surprised. "I didn't touch your stupid sweater."

"Liar!"

"Stop it," I yell, putting myself between the two of them. "Luna, go to your room."

"But . . ."

"Now!" My voice rises, and she shrinks back.

"I hate you both!" she says, tears streaming down her face as she runs back into the house.

"Mommy, why is Luna crying?" Maddox asks, running up and putting his arms around my legs.

I pick him up. "It's okay, sweetie."

"I swear, I didn't do it, Aunt Ashley."

"I believe you, honey," I say, although I'm confused to say the least. Someone cut the sweater up, and it does seem suspicious, but I don't want to make any baseless accusations. A part of me wonders if Luna could have done it to make Serena look bad. I don't know which worries me more. "Let's go inside. We'll figure this out."

Serena shakes her head. "She hates me. I shouldn't be here."

I put Maddox down and pull Serena into a hug. "She doesn't hate you. She just needs to adjust. She'll come around."

Serena gives me a skeptical look.

"I love you, Rena," Maddox says, and he hugs her.

"Let's go inside. It's almost time for dinner."

"Can I set the table?" Serena asks when we go in.

"Thanks, sweetie. That would be great."

"I'll help you," Maddox says, trailing behind her.

When we all sit down to eat, the tension is thick, and after a few failed attempts at getting a conversation going, I give up. Both girls eat quickly, not making eye contact, but Maddox chatters on, oblivious. He pushes his plate away.

"Finished. Wanna jump."

"It's chilly out, sweetie. The sun's going down."

"Please."

"I'll take him, Aunt Ashley."

Luna stands up. "I'll take him, Aunt Ashley," she mimics in a singsong voice, then throws her plate in the sink and stalks off.

Serena looks at me. "I can't do anything right." Her eyes glisten with unshed tears.

"It's not you, honey. Thanks for taking him. Just for fifteen minutes or so, okay? And grab your coats."

I think about Luna's sweater again, wondering at the culprit. Luna may have had her issues in the past, but she's never been a liar. And while Serena's been nothing but sweet, I *have* only known her for a few weeks. Sherlock pads over to me and nudges my hand with his nose. I close the dishwasher and bend down to pet him.

"What do you think, buddy?"

He stares at me with luminous brown eyes, and I kiss his head. I'm just going to have to see how things go and hope that when we start therapy, the therapist will be able to share some wisdom.

The next few hours fly by as Maddox and I do bath and story time. The girls have both retreated to their rooms for the night. By nine o'clock, I'm exhausted and turn in with my book. After a few chapters, I turn off the light and close my eyes. I don't know how long I've been asleep when the feel of the bed being bumped jolts me awake. The room is dark, but the light from the moon shines through the crack in the curtains. It takes me a moment to get my bearings, and then I see her. Serena stands at the foot of my bed, staring wordlessly as she rocks back and forth. Then, slowly, she raises her finger to her mouth.

"Shh. They're all going to die."

CHAPTER
SEVEN

I jump out of bed and run to her. She continues staring straight ahead. After a few seconds of my gently shaking her, she blinks several times then looks at me.

"Where am I?"

"My room. Are you okay?"

She shakes her head and groans. "I must have been sleepwalking again. It happens sometimes."

This has happened before? I feel torn between relief and concern.

"Let's get you back to your room."

She climbs into her own bed and pulls the covers up to her chin. "I'm sorry, Aunt Ashley. I don't usually leave my room."

"How long have you been sleepwalking?"

She shrugs. "Mom says it happens when I'm stressed. When I was younger, she put an alarm on my door but then I kind of grew out of it. Sometimes I'd just wake up and talk or do something in my room."

"Get some sleep. We can talk more about it tomorrow."

I go back to my room, grab my phone, and open a browser. I type in "sleepwalking causes" and click on the first hit. I scan the article and am relieved to see that sleepwalking is not usually a cause for alarm, and is typically outgrown by the teen years. I toss and turn for the next few hours until finally sleep overtakes me.

* * *

I'm putting the finishing touches on some photo edits when Elliott walks in. Before I can reach him, Luna comes bounding down the stairs and throws her arms around him.

"I'm so glad you're home," she says.

"Whoa. What did I do to deserve such a warm welcome?" he teases.

"Just missed you."

He comes over to me and gives me a kiss. "How about you? Did you miss me?" His blue eyes twinkle.

I shut my laptop and look up. "Always. How was the trip?"

"Fine. Made some good business connections. Excellent golf game. How's everything here?"

"Okay. I'll go upstairs with you while you unpack."

He cocks an eyebrow but says nothing.

Once we're in our bedroom and the door is shut, I sigh and sit down on the bed. "Things are worse between Luna and Serena." I tell him about the sweater. I decide not to share the sleepwalking incident for now. It's bad enough that Luna doesn't want Serena here; I don't need Elliott to start feeling that way too.

His face grows serious. "Ashley, didn't you tell me that Courtney used to destroy your stuff?"

"Not because she was trying to *hurt* me. She would get into these rages and it was like she was seeing red. I haven't seen anything like that in Serena."

His back is to me as he hangs up his suit. He shakes his head. "Well, the social worker told you she's bound to be angry and resentful. Just because she's been able to keep her temper hidden doesn't mean it's not there. Maybe she was lashing out. It's understandable considering all she's been through."

"I guess. But . . . Luna's actually the one who's been displaying anger. She's made it abundantly clear that she wishes Serena wasn't here. She's jealous of Serena having more field time in soccer. What if she did it to make Serena look bad?"

He spins around to face me. "Let's not jump to that conclusion. Luna's better now. Right?"

"Yes, but there haven't really been any stressors. She's not handling Serena's presence here very well." I shrug. "Maybe I'm blowing this out of proportion. Let's see what the therapist says tomorrow."

"Shit, I forgot about that. What time is the appointment?"

I refrain from rolling my eyes. I've only told him three times. "Noon. Remember, I made it for then so you could duck out at lunch?"

"Yeah, yeah, okay. Text me the address again."

"Okay, I'll see you downstairs."

I pass by Luna's closed door, then double back and knock.

"Who is it?" she calls.

"It's me." I open the door without waiting for an invitation. Luna's lying on her stomach, doing homework. "Hey, are you okay?"

"Not really. She's so full of it."

"What are you talking about?"

She turns to me, a storm brewing in her eyes. "Pretending to like playing with Maddox. It's just to get on your good side."

Annoyance bubbles up inside me. "Did it ever occur to you that she likes hanging out with Maddox because he's actually nice to her?"

"Whatever. Like a four-year-old has a clue. I wish she didn't live here."

"Yes, you've made that perfectly clear." I'm about to go off on a tirade but hold my tongue. I'll see what the therapist advises when Elliott and I see her tomorrow.

"She has you thinking she's so nice. You don't hear the things she says when you're not around," Luna says.

"Like what?"

"Like, one day you and Dad are gonna die and we'll be orphans too. She said everybody that you love dies."

I gasp involuntarily. "When did she say this?"

"The other day. You were outside with Maddox and she picked up a photo of the four us, turned to me, and said it."

I'm momentarily speechless. "She's traumatized, honey. Give it some time."

"She's trying to take everything that's mine. Sherlock sleeps in her room now."

"Try to be patient. Maybe having him with her makes her feel less alone."

"Whatever, Mom. You always take her side anyway."

"Now, that's not . . ."

The door bursts open and Maddox comes running in, crying and yelling.

"Mommy, ow, hurts!"

Blood is gushing from his hand. I jump from the bed and swoop him up. I yell for Elliott as I take him to the kitchen and run his hand under the sink to get a better look at the cut. It's deep, but not deep enough to require stitches.

"What happened?"

"Playing blocks." He points to the floor, where more blood has splattered.

Elliott comes rushing in. "What's going on?"

"Maddox cut himself." I point to the pile of blocks.

He goes over to examine them. "Oh my God."

"What?"

He walks over to me. "This."

He holds out a hand. Inside one of the plastic blocks is a bloody razor blade.

CHAPTER
EIGHT

Elliott and I sit in the therapist's waiting room in silence. We're both still reeling from the incident last night. Fortunately, Maddox wasn't badly hurt and a hospital visit wasn't required. My first thought had been to call the company that made the blocks and let them know what happened, but Elliott and I agreed we couldn't dismiss the possibility that Serena did it. I alerted the company just the same and they promised to investigate. The psychologist calls us in and we enter without a word. After the introductions are made and we're seated, she dives right in.

"I understand things are not going very well."

"We are concerned about some incidents." I explain to Dr. Cassidy the events of the past evening. "I'm hoping it was a manufacturing error. I can't believe Serena would do anything like that. She seems to love Maddox. The two of them have bonded beautifully."

Elliott nods. "It's disconcerting to say the least. I mean, we don't really know anything about Serena, and her mother definitely had her share of psychological problems."

Dr. Cassidy leans forward. "What kind of problems?"

I answer. "Drinking and acting out. She had a bad temper, could get violent. We want to do what's best for my niece, but we have to make sure that our children are safe."

Elliott jumps in. "It's upsetting to have our household in chaos. Our daughter, Luna, and Serena are not getting along. We're not used to all this arguing and tension."

I give Dr. Cassidy a brief history of my relationship with Courtney. "My sister and my parents were constantly at odds. She would fly into these rages." I sigh, feeling disloyal for speaking ill of her, especially now that she's gone. "She could be destructive at times."

Dr. Cassidy nods. "Family dynamics are very complicated. It's impossible for me to draw any conclusions about your sister from what you tell me. I have no idea what your parents were like, how they treated Courtney. It's best if we focus on Serena, here. Are you seeing Serena acting in way that worries you?"

I shake my head. "Not at all. In fact, she's been nothing but sweet, trying very hard to get along."

"What about what she said to Luna? About us dying?" Elliott asks.

I turn to Dr. Cassidy. "She told our daughter that everyone you love dies. Well, that's true in her case. Kids say things. Don't they?"

Dr. Cassidy purses her lips. "Serena has lost both her parents in the space of a year. Yes, I would say that her worldview right now is very dark. But that will change. She needs time and patience. I'd like to understand why you're so concerned. Aside from the incident with the sweater and the blocks, which could be totally unrelated, what other red flags have you seen to make you worried for your family?"

"Nothing," I say.

Dr. Cassidy nods. "Good. It sounds to me like Serena is having very appropriate reactions to the recent tragedies in her life. Now, I can't speak to the sweater incident, but I can see it having been done by either child, and in either case, it's not pathological. It's an immature response to jealousy. I recommend putting it in the past and working on ways to find common ground for the girls. It would be helpful to have some group sessions all together to air some of these grievances."

A nagging question makes me speak again. "What about the razor blade? If that was intentional, what would you make of that?"

"That's obviously quite serious. *If*, and I emphasize the "if," it was done deliberately, that would indicate the strong possibility of a personality disorder. I'm inclined to agree with you that it was most likely an unfortunate packaging error with the manufacturer."

"We'll follow up with the company. When should we bring the girls in for a group session?" Elliott asks.

"We can schedule something for later this week. The sooner the better. I'd also like the opportunity to speak with them individually if that's okay with you."

I nod, but Elliott shakes his head. "Why? I'm not sure I like the idea of my twelve-year-old talking to a psychologist without a parent being present."

"I understand your concern, but I just want them to feel free to express themselves without worrying about what anyone might think."

"I guess that's okay, as long as it's okay with Luna and Serena," he says.

We continue with the session, moving to more general information about trauma and grief and some things we can expect in the coming weeks. When it's time to leave, I'm just as unsettled as I was when we came in. I knew this wasn't going to be easy, but I didn't realize just how complex and difficult the road was going to be.

I'm home an hour later and Elliott goes back to his office in downtown Baltimore. Marilyn picked the boys up from preschool today and they're having a playdate at her house. She offered to bring Maddox home around five to give me some time to catch up on work. I go through my emails and respond to three queries from my website. I've been neglecting my work and I need to get back to it. I send out invoices and return phone calls. By the time I'm finished, it's close to four.

Luna and Serena must be in their rooms. I head upstairs to check on them, going first to the third floor, to Serena's room. Her door is open and she's sitting at her desk, her math book open in front of her.

"Hey there. Good day at school?" I ask.

She looks up. "Yeah."

"You need anything before dinner?"

She shakes her head.

"Okay." I turn and leave. Everything still feels forced and superficial, but I don't want to push her.

I go downstairs and am about to open Luna's door but she opens it before I can. Her face is red, her breath coming fast.

"Mom, Mom, my necklace is missing! I've looked everywhere for it!"

I walk into her room. "Are you sure?"

"Yes. I always put it right here." She points to a little box on her dresser. "I took it off yesterday to take a shower after practice. I just went to put it on now, and it's gone. She took it!"

"Whoa. Hold on. You can't just go around accusing Serena. Maybe it fell." I lean down to look under the dresser.

"Mom! I've searched the whole room. It's not here."

I sigh. "Are you sure you put it there? Sometimes when we do the same thing out of habit every day, we can think we did something and didn't. Maybe it fell off during practice?"

"It was right here!" She's screaming now.

"Take a breath." I steer her to the bed. "Breathe, in and out. Come on."

A few minutes later she's calmer.

"Check with the school tomorrow. It must have fallen off somewhere."

Could Serena have taken it? I guess it's possible, but more likely it fell off and Luna didn't realize it. Luna has always been a little too quick to blame others when things go wrong.

I go into the laundry room to move the clothes into the dryer. Until recently, we had help three days a week, but between improvements Elliott's had done to the house, the exotic vacations he plans every year, and his expensive taste in everything from cars to clothes, our spending was getting out of control. Just last summer, we spent a fortune renovating the lake house. He makes very good money, and I do okay as a freelance photographer, but I keep reminding him that it doesn't matter how much you make if your spending exceeds your income. I've tried to cut back, although as frazzled as I've been lately, I'm now second-guessing my wisdom in letting Fiona go.

My mind wanders as I pull Elliott's pants and golf shirts from the washer when something catches my eye. A key card. I pick it up. The Blake Hotel. Philadelphia. Elliott told me his conference was in Orlando. So, what the hell was he doing in Philadelphia?

CHAPTER
NINE

Elliott promised he would never cheat on me again. It had only happened once, shortly before I got pregnant with Luna. I had been working ten-hour days for Mario Ritzi, a photographer I'd long admired. Elliott was building his client list and was new to the brokerage firm, so he was putting in long hours as well. I'm not suspicious or jealous by nature, but when he got home at six in the morning after he claimed he'd been working all night, I knew something was wrong. While he was in the shower, I looked through his phone. I was relieved when I typed in his passcode and it worked. If he hadn't changed it, it must mean he had nothing to hide. I scanned his texts and saw nothing to alarm me, although it did occur to me that he could easily have deleted any incriminating messages. I scanned his photos. Nothing. Then it hit me that he might not realize his deleted photos were still accessible for thirty days. Despite his business acumen as a wealth manager, Elliott has always been somewhat of a Luddite. I navigated to the recently deleted photos and my heart sank. There, I saw a picture of a woman lying on a bed, naked except for a thick, gold collar necklace engraved with an infinity symbol. Her face was turned to the side, and only her long hair visible. I ran to the guest bathroom and vomited, then sat on the bed with his phone in my hand, waiting to confront him.

When he emerged, beads of water dripping down his chest and a towel around his waist, I shoved the phone in his face.

"What the hell, Elliott? Who is she?"

He turned pale and stammered. "How did you—"

"Answer me. Who is this? And how long have you been cheating on me?"

He sank down on the bed, shaking his head, looking at the floor. He cleared his throat several times. "It's not what you think."

"Oh really? I'm the photographer around here, not you, so why do you have a picture of some naked woman on your phone?"

"I'm so sorry, Ash. It was one night, and I barely remember it."

"Are you joking?"

"It was last month when we were at that conference in Vegas. I drank too much, and I stupidly did some E that my client gave me. It messed with my memory. I woke up in her room. She texted that picture to me, and I deleted it right away."

"So, you had sex with her? Is she a client?"

He shook his head. "She was."

"You didn't answer my question. Did you have sex with her?"

He rested his head in his hands, then looked up at me. "Apparently, from what she said. I woke up naked, but I swear, I don't remember much. The combination of ecstasy and vodka messed with my head. I would have never done it otherwise. I swear it'll never happen again. I told her I was happily married, and that was the end of it."

He promised me that he would never drink or do any drugs when he was out with clients, and although I can't verify it, he seems to have kept his word. We moved on from it and I've done my best to forget about it. But you never really move on from something like that.

By the end of the day, I can't take it anymore. As we're getting ready for bed, I go over to my dresser and pull out the key.

"Why were you in Philadelphia?"

His brow creases. "What are you talking about? I wasn't."

I open my hand and show him the key. "This was in the laundry."

Elliott takes it from me, looking at it. His expression is neutral, and he doesn't appear at all unsettled by the question. He clears his throat. "Oh, this must have been in the pocket of my Galvin Green golf pants from my business meeting a few weeks ago. You remember, I played at Cedarbrook the morning before I came home. I guess I never threw the pants in the laundry." He must see the skepticism in my eyes because he puts his arms around me. "I was in Orlando, just like I told you. I have receipts for meals from every day I was there that I'm happy to show you. I thought we got past all this a long time ago." He looks hurt.

I do remember. I feel like a fool now. "We are past it, of course. It just threw me, that's all. I didn't know what to make of it. I'm sorry."

He shakes his head. "It's okay. I made you a promise that I'd never lie to you, and I haven't." He gives me a long look. "We good?"

"Yeah," I say, but a lingering doubt remains. I can't ask him to see the receipts he claims to have, so he's off the hook unless I want to appear untrusting. I never call him at a hotel when he's away—I just call his cell phone. And his travel is all booked through his office, his charges on the company credit card, so I can't even look any of that up. It would be very easy to lie and say he was somewhere he wasn't. On the other hand, what happened was years ago and he's never given me any reason to be suspicious since. I suppose once trust is broken, it's never fully repaired.

He kisses me. A deep kiss full of promise. "Let's turn in."

I'm not in the mood.

CHAPTER
TEN

I go downstairs and open my laptop, answer some emails from earlier in the day, then follow up on some outstanding invoices. It's close to eleven by the time I'm finished, and I'm glad to see that Elliott's asleep when I come back in. After washing up, I'm about to turn out the light and get in bed when the door opens and Maddox bursts through, his face tearstained.

"Mommy, Mommy. I'm scared. There's a monster in my room. Can I sleep with you?" He runs up to me and I open my arms, hugging him to me. "Sure, sweetie." I wipe away his tears. "It's okay. It must have just been a bad dream."

He shakes his head. "No. It was real. There's a monster in my closet. I heard him."

Elliott sits up. "There's no such as thing as monsters, buddy. You can sleep with us, but let's go check out your room just so you can see it's okay."

Maddox is typically a good sleeper, but he does have occasional nightmares, and we're inclined to indulge him when he does. When I was little, I had Courtney. When we were younger, we shared a room, our twin beds pushed next to each other so we could whisper past our bedtime without anyone hearing us. Our parents were sticklers about us not bothering them through the night. Even though I was the older sister, Courtney was the one who would soothe me if I got scared or heard weird noises. She'd check around the room and show me there was nothing there. One night after I'd had a really bad dream, she sat in a chair by my bed and told me she'd wait until I fell asleep before she got back into her bed. My memories of our relationship in those early years are so fond. But once we outgrew dolls and ghost stories, the connection between us became more and more tenuous until it was almost completely gone.

Maddox starts to cry again. "No, I don't want to."

"Daddy's right, sweetie. You can sleep with us tonight, but let's go open your closet first just so you know there's no monster in there. I'm sure it was just a bad dream."

He gives me a solemn look, his brown eyes wide, and my heart breaks. He looks so sad.

Elliott gets out of bed and picks him up. "I'll carry you. Okay, buddy? You're safe."

I take a deep breath and follow them down the hall.

We go into Maddox's room and he presses his face into Elliott's shoulder, his eyes squeezed shut. The nightlight gives the room an eerie glow and the dinosaur posters and wallpaper take on an ominous feel. Elliott opens the closet door and flicks on the light.

"Nothing here, see? Just your clothes and shoes."

Maddox slowly opens his eyes and looks up.

"Now we know there's no monster. Okay?"

Maddox shakes his head. "I guess."

Elliott carries him from the room. I'm about to shut the closet door when something in the corner of the closet catches my eye. Elliott and Maddox are already in the hallway. I lean down to get a closer look. It's a leaf. I pick it up. It's wet. As though it fell from someone's shoe. But Maddox's shoes were muddy from playing outside and he took them off at the door today. Besides, he'd been asleep for hours already. Was someone in Maddox's closet tonight? And if so, who?

It's not quite dawn, but I can't fall back asleep. I make a cup of coffee and sit by the floor-to-ceiling windows in the living room. I gaze outside at the bright oranges, yellows, and reds of the leaves.

It looks like it's going to be a gorgeous October day. I love fall. The crisp, cool weather, the sense of purpose and new beginnings. But this morning, I'm filled with unease; the hotel key is all I can think about. A whining from outside jolts me from my thoughts and I go to the sliding glass door. I hear barking in the woods beyond our back yard. Stepping outside, I walk toward the noise, and as I get closer, I realize it's Sherlock. I start to run and am shocked to see him on the other side of our fence. I thought he was asleep in Serena's room.

"Sherlock, what in the world! How did you get out here?" I open the gate and he starts barking, his tail wagging, and takes off running toward the house.

Elliott is standing at the door when I approach the house. Sherlock is already inside, lapping up the water in his bowl.

"What's going on?"

"Sherlock was outside. On the other side of the fence."

"How'd he get outside?"

"I don't know. I thought he was still in Serena's room," I say.

Elliott gives me a strange look. "You don't think . . ."

"Think what?"

"Could Serena have done this?"

"Why would she do something like that?"

"Well, who else would do it?"

I shake my head. "Maybe she let him out and forgot? I don't think she'd do it on purpose. She's crazy about Sherlock." I don't tell Elliott what I'm really thinking. Luna has been jealous that Sherlock sleeps with Serena now. Maybe she did it to get Serena in trouble. But would Luna really endanger him by leaving him outside to prove a point?

I think back to when Maddox was born: Luna was seven and we tried to get her excited about the arrival of her new brother. She kept asking us to take the baby back to the hospital and insisting that she didn't want to be a big sister. Her pediatrician reassured us that jealousy was normal, especially in the beginning. We did our best to include Luna as much as possible, and when friends visited with gifts for Maddox, they brought something for her too. I thought she was finally coming around. Then, on a cold winter day, I had just put Maddox down for his nap. Luna and I were about to bake cookies when I heard a bang coming from his room. I ran into the nursery and found the French doors wide open. The wind had knocked a lamp over. The room was freezing. I grabbed Maddox and wrapped him in blankets, taking him to the kitchen. When I walked in, Luna was concentrating on decorating a sugar cookie.

"Luna! Did you open the doors in Maddox's room?"

"Uh-huh," she answered without looking up.

"Why?"

"So someone can come and take him away."

Maybe Serena isn't the one who we need to be worried about. The thought rocks me to my core.

CHAPTER
ELEVEN

I'm having lunch with Marilyn today, and I can't wait to do something that feels normal. It's so good to get away from the house, and my mood lifts in anticipation of a few drama-free hours. I park the car and walk up to Bluestone's entrance, where I feel a tap on my shoulder.

"Perfect timing," Marilyn says.

She looks immaculately put together, as usual. Her chestnut hair falls in smooth waves around her face; her creamy skin is flawless in understated makeup. She's always looked to me like the proverbial pretty girl next door. Her camel coat comes to her knees and she's wearing dark brown boots, designer, although I haven't a clue which. We link arms, go inside, and are seated.

"I don't know how you manage to look so perfect all the time," I say, marveling at the fact that her silk blouse is white, a color that is a magnet for stains any time I attempt to wear it.

She laughs. "Well, that's what a good nanny will do. I don't know why you don't get some help again, Ash. Especially now."

I shake my head. "The last thing Serena needs is another person to get used to. It's important for me to be there."

She nods, waiting until the waiter has served us our iced teas before speaking again. "Of course, I get that. It's just between your work and running a household, it's a lot. So, tell me, things still tense between Serena and Luna?"

I nod. "But I'm hopeful that after the therapy session, things might improve. Thanks for keeping Maddox when we go."

"Of course."

"One of the reasons I wanted to have lunch beforehand is that I'm a little rattled by Luna's behavior lately. I wanted to get your take on things, see how much I should bring up at the first meeting. Luna is really giving Serena a hard time. She makes hurtful comments to her and, despite my pleas, won't make any effort to include her in anything. Frankly, I'm taken aback by her lack of empathy."

"Well, Luna's always taken a while to warm up, but once she does, you couldn't have a better friend. Remember when that group of girls excluded Willow last year and Luna stood up for her? She was willing to walk away from them if they didn't treat Willow right. Luna's always had a strong moral compass. Give her some time. Maybe it would help if you back off a little, let her feel like it's her own decision instead of something you're forcing her into."

I frown. "Still. Serena's lost both her parents, and she is Luna's cousin. Shouldn't she be a bit more sympathetic? Am I missing something?"

She sighs. "Kids don't always see things the way that we do. It's got to be hard, all of a sudden, this girl she's never met is living with you. Going to her school, playing on her soccer team. Willow told me about how the coach is playing Serena more. Any kid would be upset."

I nod. "Yeah, Luna's really angry that Serena is better than her at soccer. Everything's always come so easily to her. To be honest, I've taken pride in what an overachiever she is, but maybe I've made her feel that excelling at everything is the only way to be validated."

Marilyn shakes her head. "Stop. Why do we as mothers always point the blame at ourselves? I've known you since before Luna was born. You're a terrific mother, and I've never seen you push either of your kids to do anything other than what they want to do."

Our server places our sandwiches before us. I push mine to the side. I've lost my appetite, my thoughts going dark places. Have I turned a blind eye to red flags in Luna's behavior? With the seven-year age difference between Maddox and Luna, there's been little competition at home. Luna's always been able to shine, and as the apple of Elliott's eye, she's never had to feel anything less than special. Has Serena's arrival awakened some sort of hibernating beast?

"I guess it's a good thing we're starting family therapy. Let me ask you something." I take a deep breath, then go on. "Do you think Luna could have issues I'm unaware of?"

Her brow furrows, but she shakes her head. "Like what?"

"I don't know, she's been so resentful of Serena. Do you think she might make things up to make Serena look bad?"

"What kinds of things?"

I tell her about the sweater and the missing necklace.

Marilyn shrugs. "Hard to say. It could be either of them. I don't know Serena, obviously, but the poor child has been traumatized. As for Luna, I think she's a preteen girl who's trying to manage strong emotions. These are big feelings, and she's young. I'd bring these things up in therapy. I've never had any reason to suspect anything serious. I would have told you."

When our kids were younger, I would go to Marilyn for advice. She's a psychologist with her own practice, and I respect her opinion. But once the girls were in elementary school, I was careful about what I shared. Willow was Luna's only friend back then—she had a hard time making them, and I never wanted to jeopardize that relationship. Marilyn doesn't know about the escalating temper tantrums or the hostility between Luna and Maddox. Or the incident that prompted me to take Luna to see a therapist for an evaluation two years ago. Would she have a different opinion if she knew everything?

I think back to what happened two years ago when Luna and another girl, Fern, in her Girl Scout troop were competing for the top cookie-selling prize. Luna worked her heart out and was in the lead until the day before the sale ended. Fern's father sold five hundred boxes at his law firm. Luna and some of the other girls complained that it was unethical, especially since some of the other girls in the troop had family members at the same firm. But the prize went to Fern, and Luna was inconsolable. The next day, Luna invited

Fern over after school. I was surprised but happy she was being gracious about the loss. The girls climbed up to the treehouse Elliott had built. I was looking out the window when I saw it. Luna and Fern were standing at the opening, then Luna pointed to something and suddenly pushed Fern. She fell and broke her arm. Luna swore it was an accident, and Fern, stunned by the fall, believed her. But I knew she'd done it on purpose. When I spoke to Luna about it that night, she kept denying it but finally burst into tears and admitted what she'd done. She said she was sorry, but that Fern had started bragging about winning and she got so mad, she just pushed her. She worked with a therapist on techniques to deal with frustration and impulse control for a few months until the therapist assured us she was ready to stop. Now I'm not so sure.

Elliott is late. I'm doing my best not to let the girls see how annoyed I am. Luna and Serena are sitting next to each other outside Dr. Cassidy's office, and to my delight, both are looking at Luna's phone and laughing.

"What's so funny?"

Luna doesn't look up. "An Insta reel."

I'm just glad they're actually interacting. Maybe all they needed was time. I suddenly wonder if therapy is really necessary. What if the probing and delving makes things worse, if it makes the girls focus on the difficulties? Would it be better to let nature take its course and allow them to find their own rhythm in developing a friendship?

The door opens and Dr. Cassidy asks us to come in.

I reluctantly stand. "Come on, girls." I turn to Luna. "Put your phone away."

She rolls her eyes but complies, and they follow me into the office. Still no sign of Elliott. I fire off a quick text asking where he is.

The girls sit down next to each other on the love seat, and I take a chair next to them. Dr. Cassidy sits across from us.

"Will your husband be joining us?" she asks.

I glance at my phone and see he's responded. *I'm so sorry. A client meeting got moved up. I'm not going to make it.*

I force a neutral tone. "He was planning to, but unfortunately, he got called into a meeting with his boss. I'm sorry."

She simply nods, then smiles at the girls and introduces herself.

"I'd like to start by saying I know it can feel a bit intrusive having a stranger asking you personal questions about your life. I want you to know that I'm here to be an objective advocate, something like a coach, if you will, to help resolve any issues going on in your home."

Luna and Serena are quiet and look to me as if for guidance.

"Well, I guess maybe we should talk about how you're both feeling. How about if you start, Luna?" I say.

She glares at me then looks down at her lap. "Things are okay, I guess." She shrugs her shoulders.

Dr. Cassidy lets us sit in silence and it takes everything I have not to break it. Finally Serena speaks, her voice a whisper.

"I miss my mom."

"Of course you do. And I'm so sorry for your loss," Dr. Cassidy answers. "Would you like to talk more about her?"

Serena shakes her head. "I just wish I could go home."

"I think it would be a good idea for me to spend some time with Serena alone. Would you and Luna mind waiting outside for a few minutes?" Dr. Cassidy says.

Luna and I go back to the waiting room.

"This is stupid," she says when we sit down.

"What do you mean?"

"We don't all need to be here. Serena is the one who needs to talk to a shrink. Besides, I don't hate her anymore."

I hide my surprise. "I'm glad to hear that. What's changed?"

"She's kinda cool. She showed me some of her soccer moves, helped me figure out how to defend the goal against corner kicks, and Coach noticed. I got to play half the practice."

A smile breaks out on my face. "Luna, that's great. I'm so glad to hear it."

She pulls her phone out and I'm invisible. I grab my own and look at the text Elliott sent me.

I wonder if his last-minute client meeting was just an excuse. At least he came to the first session with me.

Half an hour later the door opens, and Serena comes out. Her eyes are red, but she seems calmer somehow. She takes a seat next to Luna as Dr. Cassidy waves me inside. She shuts the door and indicates I should sit.

"That went very well. Serena's quite an impressive young lady. She's very resilient despite everything she's been through, but she's going to need all the love and support you can provide."

I nod. "Of course. I can't even imagine how hard this is for her."

"I'd like to see her twice a week for now and we'll add some family sessions in as needed. I'd still like to bring your husband in."

"Sounds good," I say, but I'm not sure that's going to happen. He's made no secret of the fact that he's not a fan of therapy. His philosophy has always been to focus on the present—he doesn't see the value in rehashing things that can't be changed.

CHAPTER
TWELVE

The therapy sessions have done wonders for Serena. There's a new lightness to her, as though a burden has lifted. After the initial meeting, Dr. Cassidy recommended that instead of coming as a family to start, that she and Serena do some grief work twice a week. It's been three weeks now, and things are still going well between Serena and Luna. Today we're all going to the farmer's market to get some pies and specialty items for Thanksgiving next week. I'm just pulling on a sweater when Elliott comes into the bedroom with a cup of coffee in his hands.

"Here you go," he says, handing it to me.

"Thanks, you're a doll. Are the kids ready?"

"Yeah, I just got Maddox dressed. He's in the kitchen with the girls."

"Things have been so calm lately, it's wonderful."

"You're right. The therapy does seem to have helped. How much longer do you think she needs to go?"

"Well, the good news is she's only going once a week now. Dr. Cassidy feels like she's processing everything much better. She still doesn't remember too much about finding Courtney or even the night before. Dr. Cassidy wants to hypnotize her, but I'm not sure about that. What do you think?"

"I don't know. That seems pretty intrusive to me. Letting someone play around in her brain? Makes me nervous. What do you think?"

"I'm leery to be honest."

He nods. "Yeah, if she's improving, maybe leave well enough alone."

When we walk into the kitchen, I'm pleased to see Luna, Serena, and Maddox working together on a jigsaw puzzle. Maddox is jumping up and down, holding a piece in his hands.

"My turn, my turn, my turn."

Luna laughs. "Okay, okay, go ahead."

I'm surprised to see Luna's wavy brown hair is now pin straight. "Luna, you have a different hairstyle today." She's never appreciated her curls, but I've always thought they suited her. Somehow, this style makes her look older.

She beams. "Serena did it for me. She has a flat iron."

"That was very nice, Serena."

"Now we look more like cousins," Luna says. Serena's blond and blue-eyed, Luna is dark-haired and brown-eyed, but they do have similar bone structure and now the identical hairstyle. Even though Serena is only a few months older than Luna, she seems more mature, and hip, for lack of a better word. Serena wears makeup, a fact that doesn't thrill me, but I've been hands off about it since I'm not her mother. But now I see that Luna's eyes are lined with black kohl, and I'm not at all happy about it.

Elliott speaks up before I can. "Luna, what's that under your eyes?"

"Eyeliner."

"Go wash it off now."

She crosses her arms in front of her chest. "Why? Serena wears it. It's not fair that she can and I can't."

"Serena is not . . ." he begins to say.

"Serena doesn't know all our rules yet," I interrupt before he can state the obvious, that Serena is not our daughter. It occurs to me in that moment that we need to remedy this sooner rather than later.

Serena can't be merely a visitor in our home. She's still a child, and if we're going to raise her with our children then she needs to have the same rules that they do. It's too soon to broach the subject of adoption, but Elliott and I need to get on the same page. Right now, we're only her foster parents, but for everyone's sake, at some point it needs to become permanent. Not just for family harmony, but for Serena as well. She has to know that she belongs to us and that no matter what, we will never abandon her.

Serena stands up. "I can wash my face. I didn't know you weren't okay with me wearing makeup."

"Well, it's just that you're both kind of young to wear makeup. Maybe we can wait until next year, you know, seventh grade, before you do?"

Luna jumps up and takes Serena's hand. "Come on, let's just go wash our faces before they have a cow."

"Luna, I don't appreciate your speaking to us that way." Elliott shakes his head and leaves too.

Maddox is on his hands and knees in front of the sofa. "Dropped puzzle piece." I look over as he slides his hand under the front of the couch and pulls something out. From where I'm standing, I can see part of a gold chain. I walk over to him.

"What do you have there, sweetie?" I whisper.

He opens his small fist, and I gasp. It's Luna's necklace. The compass charm is smashed, it looks like with a hammer or something, and the chain is broken. I take it from him and slip it into my pocket.

I hide the necklace in one of my dresser drawers, my heart pounding, dread filling me. There's no way Luna did this. First of all, she wouldn't have hidden it if she wanted to make it look as though Serena were to blame. And secondly, she'd never damage the necklace that she so cherishes. This can only mean one thing: Serena must be the one who cut the sweater and smashed the necklace. But I still can't believe she was responsible for the razor in Maddox's blocks. It makes sense that she damaged the sweater and the necklace out of jealousy, especially as, by all rights, the necklace should belong to her as the firstborn granddaughter. But what I can't understand is why she hasn't displayed any jealousy, like Luna has. It makes it all the more chilling that on the outside she is the epitome of good manners and kindness. Can she really be that cold and calculating at such a young age? I wonder now if she was really sleepwalking or if that was an act too. Why was she standing there staring at me while I slept? I need to find answers.

CHAPTER
THIRTEEN

I do my best to compose myself. I can't let anyone see how upset I am. Tomorrow is Monday, and I'll call Dr. Cassidy to tell her what's going on. Surely, she would have an inkling if Serena was dangerous. When I reach the family room, Luna is sitting on the sofa on her phone.

"Where is everyone?"

She points outside. "Maddox and Serena are on the trampoline. Dad wanted to get the leaves off the generator."

"We should get going." I open the door just as Elliott is coming toward me. I call out. "Can you get Maddox and Serena?"

He walks over to the trampoline and I watch as Maddox jumps one more time and propels himself forward. As if in slow motion, I see the netting give way and his little body fly through. I scream just as Elliott runs over and catches him before he hits the ground. I'm out the door and dashing toward them. Maddox is laughing. Serena has climbed down, her expression one of shock.

"That was fun. Do it again," Maddox says.

I grab him from Elliott and hug him to me. "What happened? How did he go through the net?"

Elliott walks over to the trampoline and examines the netting. He shakes his head. "This looks like it has been cut."

"What?" I put Maddox down and walk over.

"See?" He holds it out to show a long rip down the net. I look closer and notice some scotch tape has come loose. Elliott notices it too.

"Someone taped it so it wouldn't be noticed," he says.

"Who would do that?" Serena asks.

We both turn to look at her, saying nothing. A chill runs through me. Who is this child living in my house?

"You think I did this?" She starts to speak again, but no words come out of her mouth. She shakes her head and runs inside.

"What the hell? Why would she do that?" I say.

Elliott's eyes are wide. "If I hadn't been here, Maddox would have been seriously hurt."

Maddox tugs on my shirt. "Mommy, I taped it."

"What?"

"It was ripped. I fixed it."

"Oh, sweetie, you should have told Mommy and Daddy right away. You could have been really hurt." I look at Elliott and raise my eyebrows. "How would it rip?"

He walks over to take a closer look. "Maddox and Simon play with their trucks and cars there. Maybe somehow a sharp edge cut it.

I hope he's right. "I guess we'd better go apologize to Serena."

"You go ahead, I'll be up in a minute. I want to open the flap all the way so no one forgets and falls out."

When I get to Serena's room, the door is closed, and I knock. I hear her crying. I push the door open and she's sitting on the bed. Luna is next to her with her arm around her. Luna looks up, anger in her eyes.

"What's your guys' problem?" Luna says.

I put a hand on Serena's shoulder. "I'm sorry, Serena. We just didn't know what to think."

Luna looks at me with hostility, and Serena is quiet. She wipes her eyes then finally speaks. "I don't think I should stay here any longer."

Despite my conflicting emotions, I can't let her think she's not wanted. "Of course you should be here. You're family, and this is where you belong."

Luna nods. "You can't leave. I'm glad you're here."

Serena smiles at Luna, and I'm so grateful for this turnaround. My original instincts were right, the cousins have found friends in each other.

"I just don't know how you could think I would hurt Maddox. I would never do that. I'm trying to be a good cousin."

Luna nods. "If it wasn't for Serena, Molly Trenton would have turned all my friends against me."

"What are you talking about?"

"Molly lied and said that I told everyone that Margot Remi doesn't wear deodorant and stinks."

"She's the liar. I took her phone out of her backpack during recess and saw that she and Shannon made it up together to get Luna kicked out of the friend group," Serena says.

"That's awful."

"Now everyone's mad at Molly," Luna says with a triumphant look. "And she deserves it. She called Serena a poor orphan."

"Maybe you should tell your teacher—"

Elliott stands at the threshold and knocks. "Can I come in?"

Serena nods.

He walks over to her. "I'm so sorry for hurting your feelings, Serena. We were just so scared to see Maddox almost fall. Can you please forgive us?"

Luna squeezes her hand and after a beat, Serena slowly nods.

"Thank you. I promise we'll do better," Elliott says. But it's his work voice, the one I've heard on the phone when he's placating someone. I know he doesn't mean it. He's as torn as I am about having her here.

I take a deep breath. "Well, how about we head to the farmer's market before they've sold all their pies?"

"Okay," both girls say in unison. I turn to leave but not before I notice Serena's lip curl in a self-satisfied smile.

CHAPTER
FOURTEEN

I'm not proud of myself for what I'm doing, but I can't pretend that there's nothing wrong. The kids are all at school. I sit at Serena's desk and go through the drawers, not sure exactly what I'm looking for other than some sort of clue to her personality. I also want to see if anything else of Luna's has been taken. There are pens, paper, miscellaneous items, but nothing suspicious. Opening her dresser, I'm careful to look through her clothes and put them back the way that I found them. I methodically go through each drawer, but nothing is amiss. I go to the closet and look on the shelves, in shoeboxes, in clothing pockets, but come up empty. Moving over to her nightstand, I look through the books stacked there. I pick up the copy of *Divergent* and flip through it. Now I feel silly—I've invaded my niece's privacy for no reason. A thought occurs to me, and I lift up the mattress on her bed. Then I see it, a leather-bound book, a journal. I hesitate only a second before I slide my hand underneath and snatch it up.

Sitting on the bed, I take a deep breath and open it. A childish scrawl in black ink fills the page. I flip through. The entries take up about half of the book. I go back to the first page. There's no date, only a heading: *Feelings Journal.* I begin to read.

Today was a good day. No one could tell how mad I really was when Margaret wouldn't stop bragging about her amazing vacation. Not everyone can afford to go to Italy, Margaret. I wanted to smash her face in but I just smiled and said that sounded great. I watched everyone else's faces to see their expressions and imitated them. Sat there while she showed us her stupid pictures. When no one was looking I spilled my drink on them. Now they're ruined. Good. I hope she dies.

My blood runs cold. I have to stop for a moment as a wave of dizziness overcomes me. I flip to the next page.

Another wasted hour. Therapy is bullshit. I almost told her what I was really thinking when she asked how I was coping this week. Did the breathing exercises help? The only thing I want to do is to see her stop breathing. Nothing helps. The rage is building inside me and the only thing that stops it is imagining getting revenge on everyone who has done me wrong. I told her it helped. Smiled and thanked her. Let her check off the box that everything is good. Give me a gold star.

There's a drawing below the words. A man lying on the ground with a knife sticking out of his chest and blood everywhere. I gasp out loud.

The following entries are more of the same. Rants about the unfairness of life, how angry she is, how all she wants is to get even. By the time I get to the last entry I'm sick to my stomach.

She wants to know how I feel now that he's dead. How I'm dealing with the terrible accident. I wanted to tell her I was glad. But that would make her think I was a monster. She doesn't understand that he was the monster. The truth is that when I think about that car crashing down and crushing him to death, I'm not sad. He got what he deserved.

I put the book on the bed and take pictures of everything with my phone, including the horrible drawing. Then I put the journal back where it was. I'm numb with disbelief. I need to talk to Dr. Cassidy as soon as possible. I think about that last entry. What did she mean that her father was a monster? Was he abusing her? What the hell was going on in that house? I knew that Bobby had died in his garage while working on his Jaguar E-Type. Apparently, the jack malfunctioned and the car fell on top of him. Two accidental deaths at the house. A terrifying thought occurs to me—could Serena have killed both her parents?

CHAPTER
FIFTEEN

Marilyn brings me a cup of coffee and sits down. The boys are playing downstairs in her rec room.

"What should I do?"

She folds her hands. "Tell me again what Dr. Cassidy said?"

"That she's not seen any indication of any violence or repressed anger in Serena. Also, kids can have very strong emotions and write things in their diary that they don't mean. I asked about sociopathy but she said Serena doesn't display any of those traits."

Marilyn makes a face. "What about the picture with the knife? This doctor sounds like a quack."

"I don't think she is. She said that children can draw disturbing things when they're trying to make sense of things around them. My sister had addiction issues among other things and I think Serena was reacting to all of that. Dr. Cassidy said that her home life was very turbulent, and she believes that journal was a way for her to get her anger out."

Marilyn cocks her head. "Well, what about Sherlock being left outside? Lying about the sweater and the necklace. Now she's got Luna thinking they're best friends. Cruelty to animals, lying, manipulation." She ticks each one off on her fingers. "And if she did put a razor blade in Maddox's block and if she cut the trampoline, that's violence. I'd be very concerned. Also, that she was staring at you while you were sleeping."

"I didn't tell Dr. Cassidy about the sleepwalking or the necklace." And not even Marilyn knows that Serena said those chilling words— *They're all going to die*—the night she was standing by my bed.

She raises her eyebrows. "Why not?"

"In case Elliott ever comes to a session. I didn't tell him about those either. I was worried that he would remember all the crazy things I told him Courtney did and judge Serena unfairly. He's also got a blind spot where Luna is concerned; I was really just trying to make sure she wasn't behind things. But now of course I can see I was wrong."

"Ashley! I understand wanting to make sure Serena isn't scapegoated, but the doctor can't give you the proper advice if she doesn't have all the information. I agree that the pictures alone absent any violent behavior aren't necessarily cause for concern. But when you put them all together . . ."

I don't tell Marilyn that I'm still wondering if Luna is responsible for some of the things that have been happening. "I know, I know. I thought the necklace and the sweater were Luna's doing. But now—"

"You need to ask Dr. Cassidy to do some formal testing. And I think you should get in touch with Serena's therapist back in Pennsylvania and see what you can find out. Talk to her teachers too."

"I agree. I also want to touch base with the detective who called me about Courtney. See if he can give me the report on Bobby's death."

"Both deaths were ruled as accidents, right?"

"Yes. I did get the autopsy report on Courtney. Her blood alcohol level was above the legal limit. She'd gotten sober after she married Bobby. She wasn't drinking during those years we were still in contact. But I don't know when that changed. Obviously, she fell off the wagon at some point. She hit her head and fell into the pool. They said she was unconscious when she hit the water. She had to have been way out of it. What I can't understand is how she could let herself be so out of control with her daughter counting on her. It breaks my heart to think about what Serena has been through. It's another reason I've been desperately hoping that she's merely acting out and not a threat."

"Given her mother's issues, the trauma she's suffered, and the unstable environment in which she's been raised, there are bound to be a host of issues. That doesn't mean she can't be helped, of course. You just have to make sure that in the process your children don't become collateral damage."

"I know. I know. And that line about her father being a monster. I'm really worried about what that may mean."

She nods. "You need to speak with her old therapist and teachers. The sooner the better."

"I'm afraid to leave. What if she does something to Maddox or Luna while I'm gone?"

Marilyn drums her fingers on the table. "The Girl Scout campout next week! Instead of chaperoning with me, I'll get Ariel to take your place, and you can go then. We're leaving right after school on Friday, so you could go in the morning. Henry can pick up Maddox when he gets Simon from preschool and Elliott can get him after work."

"Okay, great."

"In the meantime, keep a close eye on her this week. I wouldn't leave Maddox alone with her, and try to monitor what she and Luna do. Hopefully I'm wrong and she's not dangerous, but until you know for sure, you need to be vigilant."

"Do you still have Simon's baby monitor?"

"Yes, why?"

"Can I borrow it?"

"Smart. Of course."

I get home with Maddox before the girls are home from soccer practice, which gives me time to hide a monitor in Luna's room. I hook up Maddox's old monitor in his. At least I'll be alerted if Serena goes into their rooms while I'm sleeping. I make some calls to plan my trip on Friday. Serena's teacher will see me in the morning, as will the school counselor, and Detective Minsk expects me right after lunch. I leave a message for Becky, the social worker, to find out the name of the therapist Serena and Courtney were seeing.

I go through the rest of the day in a semi-daze and am relieved when dinner is over and everyone has retired for the evening. Elliott had a dinner meeting and he's still not home at ten when I decide to turn in. As I slide under the covers, sleep eludes me. The words from Serena's diary make my stomach twist in knots. I vacillate between empathy for everything she's been through and fear for the well-being of my children. Have I brought a killer into our home?

CHAPTER
SIXTEEN

The drive from our house to Newtown, Pennsylvania, took a little under three hours with traffic. I'm disappointed that I won't get the opportunity to speak with the family therapist who was seeing Serena and Courtney. Her voicemail recording stated she's on vacation, so I left a message asking her to call me when she returns. I've already had three cups of coffee, and my nerves are jangling as I wait in the conference room for Serena's guidance counselor to join her homeroom teacher and me.

"How's Serena doing?" Serena's teacher, Mrs. Peterman, a young woman in her twenties, asks.

"She's adjusting. She's seeing a therapist who says she's working through the grief. I thought we were turning a corner, but I have some concerns."

Her brows rise as the door opens and another young woman joins us. I'm surprised to note the ring in her nose and the purple streak in her jet-black hair. She extends her hand.

"Morgan Winters."

"I'm Ashley Bowers."

She takes a seat and Mrs. Peterman speaks. "Mrs. Bowers was just telling me that she has some concerns regarding Serena."

Morgan shakes her head. "Such a sad situation. Losing both parents in the space of a year."

I nod. "She's been through quite a lot. And she is a lovely girl. But there have been some odd things happening." I tell them about the sweater and the necklace first. I want to ease into my admission that I read her diary. "Also, one evening the dog was left outside all night, and then there was an incident where the netting of our trampoline ripped and our son was almost hurt."

They're both looking at me now with undisguised shock. Morgan speaks. "Surely, you're not thinking that Serena is doing all of that. Who else is in the house?"

"My husband, me, and our two children. My son is four, and my daughter is twelve. At first, I thought maybe my daughter had cut the sweater because she wasn't thrilled about having Serena live with us, but she would never have damaged a family heirloom. She cherished that necklace."

"How do you think we're going to be able to help you?" Morgan asks, her tone now chilly.

"I just wanted to get a read from you. Find out if there were any behavioral issues I should be aware of, if you think it's possible Serena could be . . . troubled. I found her diary and frankly it scared me."

They both lean forward now, rapt.

I show them a few of the entries I took pictures of and wait while they read them.

"I can't believe this," Morgan says. "It doesn't sound like the same girl I knew. Serena was always very charming, actually. A bit like a little adult."

Mrs. Peterman nods. "I agree. I used to joke that she could charm the stars from the sky. Serena seemed to handle her father's death quite remarkably. In fact, there was a talent show the week after he died, and we told her we didn't expect her to participate in light of her circumstances, but she said she couldn't let her partner down. They were doing a duet. She went on like a champ."

"Um, okay. So she seemed to bounce back from his death pretty quickly, then?"

Morgan speaks up. "I wouldn't say that. Kids don't always process emotions the way adults do."

I sigh. "In light of what she wrote in her diary about his deserving to die, do you think it's possible her father was abusing her? Was there ever any indication of that? Something terrible must have happened for her to write something like that."

Morgan leans back in her chair, quiet for a long moment. "What she wrote is very disturbing. I never suspected that, and typically there are signs. But I concede that what she wrote warrants further investigation. I would bring it up with her therapist. Obviously, with both her parents gone, the only one who can tell you is Serena herself."

"For what it's worth, I met Mr. Preston on several occasions for conferences and he always struck me as a good father." Mrs. Peterman gestures with her hands. "Not that that always means something," she says.

We speak for a few more minutes and then conclude the meeting. I grab a quick lunch before my meeting with Detective Minsk. When I arrive at the police station, I'm taken to a small room where he's waiting. He stands as I come in and I'm struck once again at how tall he is. I met him last month when I came to get Serena. There's something comforting about him, a kindness in his eyes. He looks to be in his forties, so I assume he's been on the job for over twenty years, but that doesn't seem to have jaded him.

"Have a seat, Mrs. Bowers. Can I get you anything to drink?"

I shake my head. "I'm fine, thanks. I appreciate your taking the time to meet with me again."

"Of course. I trust you received the email with the police report?"

"Yes, I printed it out and brought it with me. I'm wondering, given the fact that both my sister and her husband died in accidents, was there ever any suspicion of foul play?"

He arches an eyebrow. "We never rule anything out until a full investigation is completed, but in each case, nothing suspicious was found. Just very unfortunate circumstances. As I explained last time we met, the investigation into your sister's death was pretty straight-forward." He pulls a paper from the folder in front of him. "Your brother-in-law's death was more unusual, but it was determined that he must not have secured the hydraulic jack handle tightly enough, and the jack failed." He clicks his tongue. "Unfortunate that he didn't use jack stands. You'd be surprised how many people are injured or killed by using a jack alone."

I pause, then plunge ahead. "Detective, when you spoke with my niece, how did she seem to you?"

"What do you mean?"

I hesitate, wondering if I should show him the diary entry. If it's just the frustrations of a child who was possibly abused, I don't want to raise red flags with the police and jeopardize our custody, but on the other hand, if she did have something to do with it, I have to know. I settle on a compromise. "Her teachers indicated that she didn't seem all that upset after her father died. And as you know, my sister and I have been estranged for Serena's entire life. So, I wasn't around to see how their relationship was, but she's said some things that have me wondering if it's possible her father was abusive."

He stares at me, saying nothing, and I suppress the urge to fill the silence as I wait for him to speak. He finally does. "There were never any domestic disturbances, no priors for either of them, never any report to Child Protective Services. We checked all of that when we first investigated Mr. Preston's death."

I press on. "Well, did you get a sense of anything off-kilter when you spoke with Serena after my sister's death?"

"Mrs. Bowers, she'd just lost her only remaining parent. She hardly spoke at all. Just as I would expect. Is there something you're not telling me?"

I shake my head. There's nothing he can do with a string of strange occurrences and no proof. "No, that's all. I just wanted to make sure nothing was missed." We both stand.

"Oh, one other thing," I say. "Was anyone at home when Bobby had his accident six months ago?"

He shakes his head. "No, your sister had gone to pick Serena up from school and they found him in the garage when they returned."

A chill goes through me. That means Serena witnessed two gruesome scenes.

I say thank you and leave. Before I head home, I skim the report again and a thought occurs to me. I dial Serena's old school and ask to speak with the principal.

"Hello, Mrs. Bowers? How can I help you?"

"I had one more question. Can you check the attendance records for April tenth of this year and tell me if my niece was in school that day?"

"Sure, give me a minute to pull it up on the computer. Here we go, the tenth of April you said?"

"Yes."

"No, there were no classes that day. It was a professional development day."

"Thank you."

I hang up, reeling. Courtney lied to the police. If Serena was home that day, she couldn't have left to pick her up from school. Did Serena do something to the jack to make it fail, and if so, why? And why did Courtney lie? Was she protecting Serena or herself?

I buckle my seatbelt and take my phone off silent. It's then that I see three missed calls from Marilyn. I'm about to call her when my phone rings. I glance at the screen. I don't recognize the number but I swipe.

"Hello?"

"Mrs. Bowers?"

"Yes."

"This is Janet Merrill from Girl Scout camp. I'm afraid there's been an accident."

CHAPTER
SEVENTEEN

My heart races and I blurt out, "What's happened? Is everyone all right?"

"Yes, Luna and Serena are okay. The girls were hiking near the river and one of the girls in the troop fell into the river. The leader tried to get down the rock hill but by the time she did, the current had taken her too far."

"Oh my God! Which girl? Is she okay?"

"Molly Trenton. She's in the hospital in critical condition. Obviously, we have to cut the weekend short. I'm calling all the parents to let them know. Serena and Luna are already on their way back with Marilyn Winchester."

I know Molly's mother. She must be frantic. "Thank you for letting me know. Please tell Molly's mother I'm here for anything she needs."

I call Marilyn next, and she answers on the first ring.

"Marilyn, I just heard. I can't believe—"

"You're on speaker. The girls are here."

"Oh. Hi, girls. I'm sorry to hear about Molly. Are you all okay?"

Silence.

Marilyn answers. "Everyone's shook up."

"I'll meet you at your house. What's your ETA?" I don't want to disclose the fact that I'm in Pennsylvania to Serena.

"We're going to stop and get some dinner in a bit and should be home by seven."

Great, that gives me time to get back before them. "Okay, I'll see you at your house then."

I put the car in drive and leave, shaken. Another accident in Serena's orbit. Could she have pushed Molly? I think back to the conversation I had with the girls: they said Molly was making up things about Luna and that she called Serena an orphan. All these things can't be coincidental. Dr. Cassidy agreed to do some personality tests next week, but I have to talk to Elliott now. Things are escalating, and I can't risk something worse happening.

It's six thirty when I get home, and the house is dark. I have half an hour before I need to pick up the kids, so I go inside to let Sherlock out. He's happy to see me, as always, and after he does his business, I give him some attention and then feed him. As I grab my purse, he whines, looking at me with those big brown eyes as if to say *You just got home and you're leaving again?* I lean down and kiss his head.

"I'll be right back, buddy. Don't worry."

He turns away and grabs one of his lovies from the toy basket and settles on his dog bed.

Elliott pulls up just as I'm about to get in the car. "Hey, you. Where you off to now?"

"Just picking up the kids from Marilyn's."

He frowns. "I thought they weren't coming back until tomorrow?"

"I'll explain when I get back. Marilyn's waiting for me."

"Okay."

When I pull into Marilyn's driveway, I see that her car is there. I knock at the side door and she lets me into the kitchen. She shakes her head and gives me a hug.

"Where are the kids?"

"Downstairs watching a movie. I wanted to talk to you alone."

I take a seat at the kitchen table and Marilyn puts a mug of coffee in front of me. "Any word on Molly?"

She shrugs. "Nothing yet. The water was pretty cold, and I think she was under for a few minutes. She was unconscious when they took her away in the ambulance. It's so horrible."

"How did it happen? Who was watching them?"

"We were hiking. There were twelve girls and four adults. I was at the end of the group." She rolls her eyes. "Willow didn't want me to crowd her." She puts the word "crowd" in quotes. "So, I didn't see what happened, but I know that Serena and Luna were both next to Molly, and Willow was behind them. Molly and Luna had been arguing earlier in the day and Ariel made the two of them sit down and work things out. Some issue at school last week."

I nod and fill her in on what the girls told me.

"How ridiculous. Deodorant, really? Well, Molly has always been a bit of a mean girl, but they had seemed to resolve things. Actually, Serena was the one who suggested they have lunch together and was all buddy-buddy with Molly."

"Do you think she was pushed?"

Marilyn sighs. "I mean, it's impossible for me to say. I wasn't next to them. No one saw anything, but there was a loud boom and we all turned to see what it was. It sounded like a gunshot." She shakes her head. "We never found out what it was. But it was right after that when we heard a scream, and Molly fell."

"None of the girls saw anything?"

She shakes her head.

I shudder at the idea that Serena could be capable of such an act.

"I don't know what to do," I tell her.

"I wish I had some good advice for you. I can tell you that Luna and Serena seem to have really bonded. This situation is extremely fraught."

"I know. If by some miracle all these things really are inconsequential and I then let Serena know I've suspected her, she'll never forgive me and neither will Luna. But if I continue to ignore it, who's next? I have to talk to Elliott."

I hear footsteps and talking, and everyone comes into the kitchen.

"Hi, Mommy." Maddox runs up to me. "Look what Mr. Henry got me." He holds up a Lego Batmobile that he's already put together.

I look at Henry and shake my head. "You shouldn't have. But thank you."

He smiles. "My pleasure. Your guy's a whiz at building."

"Can we go home, Mom? I'm tired," Luna says, standing next to Serena, her head resting on her cousin's shoulder.

"Of course. Get your stuff."

After we say our goodbyes, we pile into the car and drive the short distance back to our house.

"I'm really sorry about Molly," I say.

"Yeah, I hope she's okay," Serena says.

"She was so pale when they pulled her out of the water. She looked dead," Luna says.

I don't know how to respond to that. We go inside and they head off to their rooms to unpack and get ready for bed. I give Maddox a bath, read him a story, and put him down, then go to find Elliott. He's watching a show in the family room.

"So, what happened?"

"A girl almost drowned. They had to cut the trip short."

He mutes the television. "Drowned?"

I tell him what happened. "I need to talk to you about some things, but I don't want to do it here in case we're overheard. Can you go in late tomorrow so we can talk after the kids leave for school?"

"Okay, but you're worrying me."

"It's about Serena. Some things that concern me."

"Oh, okay. Tomorrow, then."

"I'm going to grab a shower then check on the girls," I say.

He nods and unmutes his show.

I go into our bedroom and turn on the monitors. Immediately, I hear a conversation between Luna and Serena. They're in Luna's room.

"Do you think anyone will find out?" Luna asks, her voice cracking.

"Don't worry. No one saw. Everything will be fine."

"You won't tell anyone what I did, right?" Luna says.

"Promise," Serena answers.

I freeze. A sense of foreboding washes over me as I remember the incident with Fern from two years ago. Did Luna push Molly?

CHAPTER
EIGHTEEN

Elliott's mouth drops open, and his face turns red. "How could you keep this from me? As soon as you read those diary entries you should have told me." He exhales. "What if it had been Luna that almost drowned?"

"But it wasn't. And Luna and Serena have been getting along great."

"I don't care. From the sound of those diary entries, Serena's emotions can turn on a dime. Smashing Luna's necklace? And now a girl who made nasty comments about her almost died? This is crazy. We have to protect our children."

"I know. That's the reason I went to Pennsylvania to see what I could find. I thought it would be safe to leave since the girls were supervised at the camping trip."

He cocks an eyebrow. "That worked out well."

"We still don't know that Serena had anything to do with it. It's very possible that Molly did fall by accident."

"And what about the conversation you heard last night? What if Serena talked Luna into doing something to get back at Molly? Maybe she made her think it was going to be a joke or something and then she pushed her off that cliff?"

I shake my head. "I don't know, Elliott. I'm really at a loss here. Both Serena's teacher and her guidance counselor had nothing but good things to say about her." I hesitate, then go on. "What if it was Luna's idea? I mean, Molly did try to turn all of her friends against her. And she made Serena promise not to tell on her."

He looks at me with incredulity. "I know Luna's had some self-control issues in the past, but she's matured since then. And after that incident with Fern, the therapist cleared her. In light of the journal and the necklace, I think we have to face facts. Serena is a very troubled child and dangerous. I don't think we can have her stay any longer. You need to call the social worker first thing tomorrow."

"I agree, but tomorrow's Saturday."

"Fine, first thing Monday. I think I should take Maddox and Luna to the lake house for the rest of the weekend and stay there until Serena's gone."

"What about school?"

"Better that they miss a few days than stay here and possibly be . . . I can't even think about it. You need to get her out of here. As soon as possible."

Elliott and the kids left about an hour ago. Luna kept asking why Serena couldn't go with them and I lied and said that she and I have to meet with the social worker for a home visit on Monday. I couldn't tell if Serena believed me, but I have to admit I feel relieved that they're gone. I'm hoping to use the time to get Serena to open up and try to determine if she had anything to do with what happened to Molly.

She comes into the kitchen as I'm ruminating on everything.

"Good morning," she says.

"Morning. Hungry?"

"A little."

"Sit down, I'll make you some eggs."

She takes a seat at the kitchen table and flips through a magazine while I cook. I bring the plate over, and my cup of coffee, and sit across from her.

"Serena, I want to talk to you about what happened at Girl Scout camp."

She looks at me with those wide blue eyes, her face the picture of innocence, and I'm struck again by her resemblance to Courtney. "Okay."

"Did you see Molly fall? Did she trip or what? I'm not clear on how it happened."

"The police asked me the same thing. I didn't see her fall. I heard that loud noise and turned around. Then I heard her scream, and she was falling when I looked back."

I decide to be forthright. "I overheard you and Luna talking. What did she mean when she asked you if anyone would find out?"

Her eyes widen in fear. "Nothing."

I reach out and put a hand on hers. "Please, tell me what's going on. If either of you have done something that could get you in trouble, I need to know."

She looks down at the table. "I promised her I wouldn't tell."

"Promised who?"

"Luna."

I stand up and go over to where my purse is sitting and reach inside. I come back to the table and open my hand. "I know about the necklace, honey. I want to help, but I can't if you won't talk to me."

She stares at me and then looks at the broken necklace. Her mouth drops open. "Oh my gosh. What happened to Luna's necklace?"

I do my best to tamp down my impatience at this innocent act. "Serena, come on. I know you did it. And I understand. You're the oldest granddaughter, it should have gone to you, but as I said, I can't help if you won't be honest with me."

Tears spring to her eyes, and she bounds out of her chair. "I didn't do that! How could you think I did that?"

"I'm sorry, but—"

She runs from the room. I'm about to go after her when my phone rings. I glance at the screen. It's the therapist's office in Pennsylvania. I can't miss this call.

"Hello?"

"Mrs. Bowers?"

"Yes, this is she."

"This is Dr. Fairway returning your call. What can I do for you?"

"I'm Courtney's sister. Her daughter, Serena, is living with us. I found some diary entries of hers that have made me very concerned about the safety of our family. I know you treated Serena and wanted to know if you think she could be dangerous."

"I never treated Serena."

"But the social worker said you were seeing Courtney and Serena together. Her diary mentions that you're the one who suggested she keep a feelings journal."

"I was seeing only your sister. It must be her journal you're talking about."

I clutch the phone tighter. "Oh my God! The journal was Courtney's? But the handwriting is so messy and childlike."

"Normally I wouldn't disclose anything about a patient, but since your sister is deceased, and you are caring for her child, I don't suppose it will hurt. All I can tell you is that your sister was on several medications, some of which affect handwriting."

"She sounded so angry and full of rage."

"I'm really not comfortable commenting any further."

"Thank you," I say and hang up, relief flooding me. But my relief is short-lived. There are still so many other unexplained incidents, not the least of which is what happened to Molly, and whatever it is Serena won't tell me.

CHAPTER NINETEEN

Now that I know the diary wasn't Serena's, I have to rethink everything. I knock on her door, and she mumbles for me to come in. I feel terrible when I open the door and see her lying on the bed, her eyes red, crying.

"Serena, I'm so sorry. Can you ever forgive me? I was wrong to accuse you. I don't understand why these things are happening."

"I thought that I was finally going to be a part of a normal family. But I guess I don't belong here." Her lip trembles. "I don't belong anywhere."

"No, no. That's not true. Honey, I'm so sorry. None of this is your fault. I know you must miss your mom and dad terribly, and I feel horrible that I've made you feel unwelcome by accusing you of those things."

"I miss them, but things were bad sometimes. My mom would get really mad and break things. It was scary."

"I think your mom needed help, sweetheart. Did she ever hurt you?"

She shakes her head. "No, but she and my dad fought all the time. Then after he died, she was drinking a lot. I pretty much had to take care of myself."

"Well, I promise you, you're safe here."

"Aunt Ashley, if I tell you what happened at camp, do you promise not to get mad at Luna?"

"I can't promise that without knowing what it is, but I can promise to do my best to understand."

She bites her lip. "Okay, well. You know Molly has been really mean to Luna, right? And after Mrs. Miller made us all talk, we thought everything was okay."

"Go on."

"Except afterward Molly called her a tattletale and said she was going to tell everyone what a baby Luna was. So . . . Luna found some ants and snuck into Molly's tent. She put them in the pockets of her jacket right before the hike."

I'm momentarily confused. That seems like a harmless prank. But then it hits me. "Wait, are you saying you think the ants scared Molly, and that's why she fell?"

She starts to cry again. "What if they did?"

I'm not sure what to say. "Maybe the noise you all heard startled her. We don't know what happened, but what I do know is that neither you nor Luna meant to hurt her. You can't blame yourselves. I'll talk to Luna when she gets back."

She nods. "Okay."

"Listen, kiddo. Why don't we go out for some ice cream? I think we could both use some cheering up."

We drive to the ice cream shop a few miles from our house. Serena orders a double chocolate cone, and I get a cup of vanilla.

"Want to grab a booth or take it with us?" she asks.

"Let's sit. I'm really happy that you and Luna have gotten so close," I say.

She smiles. "I always wished I had a sister. Were you and my mom ever close?"

I lean back and sigh. "Yes. We were. We were always very different, but I tried to look out for her. She could be . . . difficult sometimes. But I loved her very much."

"She said you stole her money. Now that I know you, I find it hard to believe."

"I didn't steal it. Our parents did a bad thing. They cut your mom out of their will. I offered to give her half the money, but she was so hurt that she wouldn't take it." I don't tell her that I put it in a trust and her father squandered it. I don't want her memories of her father to be tainted. I shake my head. "It doesn't matter now. But I want you to know that I loved your mother, and I deeply regret that we didn't speak for all those years. I'm just happy that Maddox and Luna get to be with their cousin. And I get to be with my niece." I smile at her.

"I'm glad too."

CHAPTER
TWENTY

I called Elliott after my talk with Serena yesterday to fill him in on everything I learned. He and the kids came back this morning. The first thing Luna did when they got home was run to find Serena. I dropped Maddox off at Marilyn's, then took the girls to the mall so that Elliott and I could talk. We go to the bookstore coffee shop and grab a table.

"I'll admit it's a relief that she didn't write those horrible journal entries. But she *was* raised by someone who did. I'm not convinced we're really out of the woods here," he says.

"I don't disagree. But I don't think she's dangerous. And she and Luna love each other. In fact, she's been nothing but supportive of Luna. Whatever happened with the sweater and the necklace, that's unimportant now."

"I don't know, Ash. I still think she's the one who put Sherlock outside. The trampoline, the razor. Maybe she's calm right now but what if something happens to trigger her? I don't think she's stable."

"Well, the trampoline was ripped, right? And I just have to believe the razor was a manufacturing error."

He tilts his head. "Maybe. But what about Sherlock?"

"I really think that was Luna. But again, I think we just move forward now. Dr. Cassidy thinks Serena is doing well. She has a lot to deal with between her parents' deaths and the fact that she read all those horrible things in Courtney's journal. Dr. Cassidy is helping her to work through all that. I think she's actually quite a remarkable girl to be so positive and sweet in light of all she's been through."

He takes a sip from his coffee, then shakes his head. "You always see only what you want to see. You were the same way with Courtney. You're doing it again with Serena. Remember what happened at your bachelorette party?"

How could I forget? Courtney was angry because my wedding reception was at our parents' country club and hers wasn't. But she gave them only two months' notice while I gave them a year, and there was no opening on the schedule for her wedding. I did wonder at the time if my mother lied about that because she was worried that Courtney might start drinking again and embarrass her. Courtney could be vicious when she had too much alcohol. Regardless, it was just more evidence in her mind that I was the favorite.

I asked her to be my maid of honor, as I'd been hers. She threw me a beautiful shower, came to all the dress fittings, helped me with last-minute errands—everything was great. I told her that I wanted something low-key for the bachelorette party. I especially didn't want to go barhopping and tempt Courtney to drink. She'd been sober for almost a year at that point. I was nervous when I saw the champagne in the limo, but she abstained. The night started out exactly as I'd hoped. We had dinner at the Prime Rib, then were going to head home. But the other bridesmaids wanted to go to a few bars, and Courtney said she was fine with it. Courtney kept ordering me vodka and sodas, telling me she was living vicariously through me. I got wasted. I've never been a big drinker. By the end of the night, I was barely able to walk on my own. Courtney talked us into going to an after-hours club on the Block, downtown Baltimore's red-light district, and it just happened to get raided that evening. Only because of my father's connections were we released from the police station without being charged.

The next morning, the first thing Courtney said to me was, "How does it feel to be the one in trouble for a change?"

"I'll admit, trouble seemed to find Courtney," I say to Elliott. "I was furious after that night, but she was sorry. And she never did anything like that again. You remember, the four of us were very close. Until my parents . . ."

"My point is, she was reckless and did things that put you in jeopardy. She would lull you into a false sense of security, you'd think everything was fine, and then something would come up to make her jealous and she'd lash out."

"I was to blame as well, Elliott. She didn't pour those drinks down my throat. And why are we rehashing all this anyhow? As I keep saying, Serena is not Courtney."

"The sins of the mother," he says, barely under his breath.

"Do you really think it's fair to blame Serena for things she had nothing to do with?"

He sighs. "No, you're right. I feel bad for all she's been through, and I know it's not her fault. She can stay. But let's be on high alert. As much as I want to help her, I won't jeopardize Maddox's and Luna's safety."

"I hear you. Everything will be fine. You'll see."

CHAPTER
TWENTY-ONE

Christmas is two weeks away, but first, we have Luna's birthday to celebrate. Her party is today. I suggested a sleepover, but apparently that is "so last year." Instead, we're having a spa-themed party where a mobile business will come over and set up mani/pedi and facial stations. I'm on my second cup of coffee when Luna comes into the kitchen, still half asleep.

"Happy birthday, teenager." I stand up and give her a hug.

"Thanks."

"Do you feel older?" I tease.

She shakes her head. "Not really. Did everything come in for the party favors?"

The goody bags are spa themed, with nail polish, manicure kits, a coupon for a manicure, and personalized eye masks with everyone's names. The masks were ordered online and arrived yesterday. "Yes, all set. They're over there on the counter." I point.

Luna gets up and opens one, looking through. "Very cool. Thanks, Mom."

"Happy birthday, Luna," Serena says, walking in holding a gift bag.

"Thanks," Luna says, giving her a hug. "What's this?"

"I wanted to give you your present early."

Luna pushes the tissue paper aside and pulls out a canvas. "Oh my gosh! Serena, this is so cool. I love it!" She turns it around so I can see. It's a charcoal drawing of Luna. Serena has really captured Luna's essence. It's brilliant.

"Oh, Serena. It's absolutely beautiful. You are so talented," I say.

She blushes. "I was taking lessons."

"Oh, I didn't know that! Would you like to continue?" I ask.

"I can't ask you to pay for that."

"Nonsense. We're happy to. We'll look into it next week."

"Thanks. But today's Luna's day." She smiles at Luna. "Now we're the same age."

"What did you do for your thirteenth?" Luna asks her.

Serena gets a faraway look in her eyes. "Not much. My dad brought home a cake."

The room becomes quiet. I make my voice bright. "Well, let me make a very special breakfast for the two of you. French toast or chocolate chip pancakes?"

"Let the birthday girl decide," Serena says, her voice flat.

Hours later, the house is buzzing with the excited chatter of twelve girls. Molly made a full recovery and you'd never know that there was any animosity between her and Luna. Luna has been bending over backward to be nice to her—partly from guilt, I believe, but I'm just glad that things turned out okay. Elliott took Maddox out for the day and I've stayed mainly in the kitchen and out of the way, just there to dole out drinks and snacks, then pizza. It's almost time for presents and cake, and I'm relieved that the party has gone so well. Luna is having the time of her life.

"Is it safe to come in?" Elliott says as he and Maddox come into the kitchen.

I laugh. "Yes. The mobile spa folks are gone and the girls are almost finished watching *13 Going on 30* while having pizza. Should be ready for presents and cake soon."

"Good. I wanted to make sure we were back to sing to her."

"Cake, cake!" Maddox says.

"Not yet, babe. Soon."

The two of them go outside, and Maddox plays on the swings. About twenty minutes later, I hear the girls coming upstairs from the rec room.

"Ready for cake?"

Luna nods.

"I'll bring it all into the dining room."

I call Maddox and Elliott in. He lights the candles on the cake, and we take it to the girls, singing "Happy Birthday."

"Make a wish," I say. Luna closes her eyes, then opens them and blows out the candles. Elliott and I hand out cake, then sit back while the girls chat and eat. Next are presents, and I take notes as Luna gleefully rips open each package so she can write thank-you notes later. I glance at Serena, who is watching Luna. I try to discern her expression—she seems sad, but I don't know her well enough to be sure. It must be painful for her to watch her cousin celebrated by her family and friends knowing that she'll never again have a birthday with her parents.

It's finally time for everyone to leave, and I'm eager for them to go. Luna hands out the goody bags, and I'm ready to breathe a sigh of relief when her friend Tara yells out, "Ewww, what is this?"

She holds her hand out and there is something red and sticky all over it. The other girls open their bags and suddenly there are shouts of "It's all red!" and "Gross!"

It looks like blood.

I run over and grab the bag from Tara's hand. I peer inside and see that the contents are covered by the thick substance. I think it's ketchup. I hold the bag to my nose and confirm that it is. Someone has poured ketchup all over the contents in the goody bags.

"Girls, I'm so sorry," I say. "It's only ketchup. Go wash your hands, and I'll order new bags for you. I don't know how this happened."

"I do!"

I look over and Luna's face is red, and tears are streaming down her face. She points at Serena. "Why did you do this? I thought you were my friend!" She runs from the room and up the stairs.

Serena has turned white. "I didn't do it." She looks at me. "I swear, Aunt Ashley, it wasn't me."

I usher the girls from the house, heartsick. Luna's birthday has been ruined, and she's humiliated. Everyone at school will be talking about it. There's no doubt in my mind now that it's been Serena all along. She has to go.

I told her as gently as I could that things were not going to work out. I'll never forget the devastated look on her face or the words that ripped through my heart. "You're kicking me out? Where will I live?" She swore that she hadn't been the one to do it, but I can't believe her anymore. This morning, I woke up before Serena and called the social worker; we're going to meet her later this afternoon. I feel like I've failed everyone.

I see the postal truck pull up and go to retrieve my mail. After I pour myself another cup of coffee, I sort through it and stop when I see a manila envelope with an attorney's return address. I tear it open.

Dear Mrs. Bowers,

Your sister came to see me a few months ago. She was preparing to initiate a lawsuit for child support. She informed me that she was going to speak to the father on her own, but if he didn't agree, then she wanted me to file a suit. I didn't hear from her again and thought she had resolved the situation on her own until I read news of her death. I got your contact number from the police. I have provided the information contained herein to them as well as I believe it may have some bearing on her death. Enclosed is a DNA test identifying the father of her minor child, Serena Preston.

Very truly yours,

Malcom Weathersfield, Esq.

I'm gobsmacked. Bobby wasn't Serena's father? I can't believe Courtney was cheating on him. My eyes go to the box with the name of Serena's biological father and my heart stops as they fixate on the name typed there: Elliott Bowers.

CHAPTER
TWENTY-TWO

Elliott is Serena's father! The words play over and over in my head. My husband slept with my sister. My head is spinning, and I feel sick. How can this be? Were they having a long-term affair? Did Bobby know? Does Elliott even know that he's Serena's father? I can't make sense of this. And now I wonder if this is the real reason my sister and I have been estranged all these years. It's inconceivable. Who is this man that I've spent the past seventeen years with?

I think back to when he had that one-night stand. It was over thirteen years ago. The woman in the picture. Could it be? I open my phone and navigate to the invisible app on it. Years ago, I texted the picture of the woman I found on Elliott's phone to myself. I enlarge the photo, taking in all the details I was too devastated to look at before. I can't see her face in the picture; she's on her side, her long blond hair covering her face on the pillow. Then I notice the strawberry birthmark right above her ankle. It's small, small enough not to stand out unless you're looking for it. The woman is definitely Courtney. I'm heartsick as the truth dawns on me. Elliott and my sister had sex. And the timing works. It would have been around nine months before Serena was born.

Another thought occurs to me. I retrieve the key card I found in his pants and call the hotel. When I reach the front desk, I speak.

"This is Missy Barnes, Elliott Bower's admin," I lie. "I'm missing some receipts for his expense report. Can you please look his name up, then email me any receipts from stays in the past six months?"

"Yes, ma'am, please hold a moment and I'll take a look."

I drum my fingers on the table while I wait. After a few minutes, he comes back on the line. "Yes, there was just one stay in the past six months. It was on October second."

"Thank you, please email it to Abowersphoto@gmail.com."

He repeats the email address and we finish the call.

Moments later, the receipt is on my phone.

What else is my bastard husband hiding? I go into his office and turn on his desktop. After everything loads, it asks for a password. I try several to no avail. An idea strikes me. Elliott is always forgetting all his passwords. I open the password book in the top drawer, and go to the Cs. Voila! "Computer password" is there.

Elliott's internet browser is open and I can see that he has a ton of open tabs. His computer skills are abysmal. I click on the first one—*Characteristics of a sociopathic child*. He must have been really worried to be looking this up. The other tabs are more of the same. I click on the last one and my blood runs cold. It's a case study of an eleven-year-old child who cut up her sister's clothes, broke a piece of jewelry, put a razor blade in a toy, cut the netting on the trampoline, and left the family pet outside all night. It's a blueprint for everything that happened, and suddenly it hits me with such clarity and force that I can't catch my breath. Elliott. He's the one doing it all. I go through more folders on his desktop, articles he's saved, research he's done. My blood runs cold when I open the one named *High School*.

I leave the office and go back to the kitchen, sinking down into a chair, then I call Marilyn and tell her what I've found.

"I can't believe it! Elliott's been behind everything?" she says.

"There's more. He's Serena's father."

"What?"

I tell her about the letter from the attorney. "I guess he wanted to get rid of Serena in case somehow I found out." I don't tell her what else I've discovered. I can't risk anyone knowing until everything is in place. "He took the kids to the lake house. He thinks I'm taking Serena back to Pennsylvania today. I mean, I was, but now . . . I have to find out what the hell is going on. I'm going to tell him she's gone and to come back tomorrow. Can I drop Serena off with you in the morning? I'm going to confront him when he gets back."

"Of course. But what if he's dangerous? To do the things he's done, he's sick."

"He's not going to do anything to me."

"How do you know? Listen to me, Ashley. This is what I do for a living. Your husband is clearly disturbed. To frame that poor child just to get out of raising her is unfathomable. Especially since he's her father. This is unbelievable! Don't forget this means he was the one who put the razor in Maddox's toy. He could have seriously hurt or even killed his own son."

"I know. It's insane. I don't understand, but I have to find out why. Trust me. Nothing's going to happen to me."

We hang up, and I call the social worker to let her know I don't need to meet with her after all.

I go upstairs to find Serena. I don't know what I'm going to tell her, other than the fact that I believe she had nothing to do with the incident at the birthday party. Her door is shut and I knock. No answer. I knock again and wait. Finally, I push the door open. The closet door is open and some of her clothes are gone. She must have snuck out last night. I can't blame her. How many times have we accused her, only to apologize later? She's been horribly scapegoated. I look around to see if she left a note, but there's nothing. I have to find Serena. I tear out of the room, grab my car keys, and jump into the SUV. All sorts of horrible thoughts go through my mind. What if she hitchhiked and the wrong person picked her up? Plus, it's freezing outside. I'll never forgive myself if something happens to her.

CHAPTER
TWENTY-THREE

I drive down Shawan Road, looking to my left and right, passing woods, fields, livestock. My heart is racing. I say a prayer as I frantically look for any sign of Serena. I drive for the next half hour, but she's nowhere to be found. I head back to the house, ready to call the police, when my phone rings.

"Mrs. Bowers?"

"Yes?"

"This is Sergeant Valentine. We have your niece here at the Baltimore County Police Department."

"Oh, thank God! Is she okay?"

"Yes, an officer stopped when he saw her hitchhiking late last night on York Road. She wouldn't give us any information until just now. Someone from CPS is with her."

"I'll be right there to pick her up." I end the call and turn back around. I hope CPS will release her into my custody. And what am I going to say to Serena? I call Marilyn on the way and apprise her of the situation.

"She ran away? Thank God she wasn't hurt or kidnapped."

"I know. What should I say? I can't tell her that Elliott did all this, especially in front of a social worker. They'll never let me take her."

"Try to say as little as possible. She ran away, it's been an adjustment, she's in therapy. When you're alone with Serena you can apologize and tell her you're going to deal with everything."

"Okay."

Four hours later, after a lengthy discussion with the social worker and a call with Dr. Cassidy, Serena and I are on our way back home.

"I can't stay with you. You accused me of doing all those awful things."

"I know, and I'm so sorry. But I'll explain everything soon. And you'll understand. The only thing I can tell you right now is that I know for a fact that you did none of those things. I promise, no one will ever accuse you again."

CHAPTER
TWENTY-FOUR

I've been on pins and needles ever since Elliott came home. I dropped Serena off with Marilyn early this morning, and her husband came to pick up Maddox and Luna half an hour ago. I can't have this conversation with Elliott while the kids are in the house. I pour myself a cup of coffee with a shaking hand, anxious to get this over with. It was torture, kissing him hello, pretending that everything was fine.

He comes into the kitchen, his salt-and-pepper hair still wet from the shower, his handsome face wearing a look of concern. "I'm sure it was hard on you, but I'm glad Serena is gone. It was the only thing to do."

I want to spit in his face but say nothing.

He walks toward me and puts his arms around me. It takes everything in me not to cringe. "I know it's hard, Ash. But it's for the best. We have to think about the safety of our kids."

"I want to talk to you about that. Let's sit."

"Okay." He pulls out a chair and sits across from me.

"You see, I got something very interesting in the mail yesterday."

"What?"

"A paternity test. It seems that Bobby wasn't Serena's father."

A look of shock crosses his face, but I can see he's feigning it. "Seriously?"

"Yes." I grab the folder from the chair next to me and slide it across the table. "You are."

His face turns white as he opens the folder, his eyes scanning the report. He clears his throat. "Is this some sort of a trick? What the hell?"

"It's not a trick, you son of a bitch. You slept with my sister. How long was it going on? Are you the reason she didn't speak to me for all these years?" Images of my sister flash through my mind. Pictures of us as little girls, then teens, and then those precious years after we were both first married and still close. He stole my sister from me. All those years of heartache and longing should never have happened. He took so much from both of us. "Hate" is too weak a word for what I feel for him.

"No, no. Of course not. It was nothing like that. Let me explain."

I scoff. "You're not going to bullshit your way out of this one, you lying snake."

"It was only one time. I swear."

"When?"

"A few months after your parents died. She called wanting some financial advice. She asked me not to tell you. Bobby was out of town and one thing led to another."

I'm incredulous. "One thing led to another? She was my sister! What kind of person does that?"

"She was upset about the will, was crying, I went to comfort her and—"

"Stop lying. You raped her."

He shrinks back as though I've struck him.

"What?"

"I called her therapist. I had a feeling something was off when I looked at that picture again. She looked drugged—"

"What pic—"

"Shut up. Let me finish. When I told her therapist I knew who assaulted her, she admitted it. She broke confidentiality out of concern for me when I told her I was married to you. You ruined her life, do you know that? Her therapist told me that Courtney called our house that day. She wanted to make up with me. She was ready to take half of the inheritance. And you lied and told her you'd bring the paperwork. You lured her to your hotel room, then you drugged and raped her. She woke up in your bed the next morning with no recollection of anything after the drink you gave her. What I don't understand is *why*?"

"She was drunk. She knew what she was doing."

"Bullshit. Her therapist told me she'd been sober for years until after that night."

"Yeah, well, all I can tell you is that she must have started drinking again. Because she gladly accepted the whiskey I poured her."

"What else was in the glass besides whiskey? It's a pattern with you. I know what happened when you were in high school."

He stammers, "How do you—"

"I found the articles you saved, accusing you of rape. You've gotten away with two rapes now. Don't bother denying it. Why did you rape my sister?"

It's as though a mask has dropped, and I can see the real him for the first time. He looks feral. The blankness in his eyes is terrifying. "Why do you think? She wanted the money. Your parents left it to you. There was no way I was going to give up a million and a half to her. For what? So yeah, maybe I did put something in her drink. But it's not like she didn't want it. She was always flirting with me. When she woke up the next morning, I showed her the picture and told her I'd tell Bobby. I warned her to stay away from you and to forget about asking for that money."

"How could you do that?" I push his chest as hard as I can, wanting to kill him. "Who the hell are you? As if that wasn't enough, you've been gaslighting all of us. You put the razor in Maddox's blocks. How could you do those things?"

"I didn't—"

I put my hand up. "Stop. I found all your research on your computer. I know you did it. Serena's your daughter. Doesn't that mean anything to you?"

His eyes narrow. "Your bitch sister was blackmailing me. Did you know that? I had no idea Serena was mine until a few months ago, after Bobby died and she was broke. The idiot went through all her money. She called me for help after he died and I gave her fifty grand. That must have been when she got my DNA on a glass or whatever. She lured me there for that reason. Then when she found out that I was Serena's father, she wanted more. She would have bled us dry."

I pull out my trump card next. "Is that why you went to see her the night she died? Did you kill her?"

"Wait. How do you—"

"The key card you left in your pants. I called the Blake Hotel. Turns out you stayed there the night she died. They sent me a copy of the receipt."

He puts his head in his hands, shaking his head back and forth. "It was an accident. I swear. She was drunk. Wouldn't listen to reason. She threatened to tell you. I couldn't let that happen. She dialed you on her phone, and I went to grab the phone from her. We struggled and she fell and hit her head."

"Did you push her into the pool?"

He doesn't answer, just looks straight ahead. "Before I left, I looked up and Serena was staring out of her bedroom window. I don't know why she didn't say anything or if she was in shock, but I was afraid the longer she was with us, the more likely she would remember."

I think of the night she was standing at the foot of my bed. "She sleepwalks. She probably didn't even see you. But you didn't answer my question. You pushed her into the pool, didn't you? Just let her drown. How could you do that?"

"I wasn't going to let her ruin my family because her husband gambled away all their money. She would have told you everything. I couldn't let that happen."

I look at this man I thought I knew and realize he's a complete stranger. How could I have lived with him all this time and not seen the monster inside him? "You have to go to the police."

His eyes widen. "Are you crazy? What's the point? It won't bring her back. And if Serena was asleep and really didn't see me, she can stay. We can still be a family."

"Are you insane? We're finished. You're going to prison, and you will never come near Serena or my children again."

"Be reasonable, Ashley. There's no proof. If you say anything to the police, I'll just deny it, and then I'll fight you for custody. And Serena's mine." He holds up the report. "The DNA proves it, so your precious niece will have nothing to do with *you*, if you stir up any trouble."

"You honestly think I'm going to stay married to you after all you've done? You're a murderer."

"Good luck proving it."

"Did you get all that?"

He looks at me, and then around the room. "What? Who are you talking to?"

The front doorbell rings and I get up. "That'll be the police. Our entire conversation has been recorded."

He lunges for me, but I'm prepared. I pull the pepper spray gun from my pocket and pull the trigger, aiming for his eyes. He howls in pain, and I run to the door. Detective Minsk and another detective rush in.

Elliott's eyes are blood red and tears run down his face as he stumbles to steady himself at the counter. Detective Minsk reads him his rights and cuffs him.

Elliott looks at me in shock. "You turned me in? How could you do that? What about our family?"

I shake my head. "Our family doesn't include you any longer."

CHAPTER
TWENTY-FIVE

One Year Later

It's been a rough road, but we're well on our way to healing. Dr. Cassidy has been a miracle worker. After our family imploded and Elliott went to prison, I didn't know how we were all going to get through it. There are so many layers to this heartbreak. For Luna, finding out that the man she adored, who seemed to adore her, was the one behind all those despicable actions put her into a deep depression. I shielded her from the press and the trial as much as I could, but these days, nothing is hidden, and it's impossible to protect your kids from the news. And Serena, poor child, first to find out that Bobby wasn't her biological father, and that Elliott, who was, murdered her mother. Serena has also had to process that even though Elliott knew he was her father, he tried his best to discredit her and make her out to be seriously disturbed. The one bright spot in this mess is that Serena and Luna are truly sisters and they've clung to each other, becoming closer every day. Maddox, blessedly, is still young enough to be much less affected.

I was still worried that maybe Courtney had something to do with Bobby's death, especially since I thought she'd lied about Serena being in school that day. But it turns out, she was in art class, and that's where Courtney had picked her up. Bobby's death was a tragic accident, and Courtney's anger at him had nothing to do with paternity or abuse, but with the fact that he'd lost all their money. He died not knowing that Serena wasn't his biological daughter. And Courtney, my tortured sister, worked so hard to get her life together only to have it torn apart by Elliott's horrendous actions. I'll never know whether she really did start drinking again or if Elliott drugged a glass of something non-alcoholic and made her believe she'd taken a drink of her own free will the night that he assaulted her. What I do know is that he set her on the course to self-destruction. It's no wonder she never told me the truth; he used shame and humiliation to make her believe she wasn't worthy of my love anymore.

Now it's time to put the past behind us and look ahead. I decided to sell the house and move somewhere we can make a fresh start. A place where whispers don't follow us everywhere we go and my children can find peace. We're all ready for a change.

The moving van has just pulled away, and the kids are saying their goodbyes to Willow and Simon.

Marilyn looks at me, her eyes brimming with tears. "I'm going to miss you so much."

"I'll miss you too. You've been my rock through all this. But you'll come visit. Often, right?"

"You betcha. Especially when it's freezing here, and you're all lounging by the pool in sunny Scottsdale."

"Plan to come over winter break," I say, trying to stay strong but ready to break down. "I hope I'm doing the right thing. It's so far." When we were discussing where to go, both girls begged for somewhere warm. I thought about Florida at first, wanting to stay on the east coast, but when I got a call from Mario, who lives in Scottsdale, asking if I'd be interested in working with him again, it felt like it was fate. So, we're taking a leap of faith.

"As much as I hate to see you go, I think it's the right thing for everyone."

"I thought at first the kids would want to visit Elliott in prison, but Luna wants nothing to do with him, and not surprisingly, Serena doesn't either. Maddox is too young, and I wouldn't want to expose him to that environment. But I do feel bad, taking them so far away."

She shakes her head. "Elliott gave up his right to be a father to them when he did all those horrible things. You have a good heart, but the kids are much better off without him in their lives."

I know she's right. I still can't get my head around the fact that he killed my sister. All the things he did were the desperate acts of a man terrified of being exposed. I can't help but wonder: If he'd never raped Courtney and started this whole chain of events, would I have lived the rest of my life with him, completely oblivious to his true character and what he's capable of? That thought scares the hell out of me.

I look outside at all the kids. They're sitting in a circle on the trampoline, laughing and chatting, and a sense of melancholy fills me. I hope we'll be able to find friends even half as loyal as these. Marilyn and I step outside.

"Time to shove off," I say. Maddox and Simon scramble down first, then the three girls. Sherlock jumps into the back hatch of our car, his tail wagging furiously. There are hugs and tears and promises to stay in touch. After Marilyn drives off, we get into the SUV.

"Everybody buckle up."

I put it in drive, and we head out into our new adventure.

SILENT ECHO

To Rick,
For always doing your best to soothe this mother's worrying heart
and so much more. xo

PROLOGUE

The day began like any other. Charlotte Fleming grabbed her coffee from the kitchen and rushed into her son's room, cursing as the hot liquid sloshed from the mug and stained her silk shirt. Shit, now she was going to be late.

"Sebastion, come on, we need to get a move on," she called as she raced down the hallway.

No response from her four-year-old son. Exasperated, she walked into his room and saw he was still in bed.

"Sebastion! Why aren't you up? We have to leave for school."

He looked up at her, his blue eyes wide. "My tummy hurts."

Not this again, she thought. Ever since she'd gone back to work full-time, Sebastion had been complaining of phantom illnesses. They'd made several trips to the pediatrician, and there was nothing wrong each time. She wasn't unsympathetic. She hated being away from him for so many hours every day, but today, she couldn't coddle him. Of all days for Eli to have a job interview. She sighed, walked over to the bed, and sat on the side. She put a hand on his forehead. He didn't feel warm.

"Honey, you don't have a fever. And you've been looking forward to the field trip all week. Do you think you're just hungry?"

He shook his head, his blond curls catching the sunlight. "I wanna stay home."

"Does it hurt here?" She pressed on his side, and he shook his head. "Tell you what, special treat, you can eat a Pop-Tart on the way to school and see if you feel better." A stab of guilt pierced her for bribing him, but she couldn't miss her client meeting this morning.

"Okay, Mommy." He slid from under the covers and she helped him dress quickly, then ran to her room to change her blouse. She grabbed her briefcase, a strawberry Pop-Tart, and a juice box, and they flew out the door. As she drove, she glanced in the rearview mirror and was relieved to see him eating. He was fine. If Eli landed the job today, that would take the pressure off her. She could scale back her hours and spend more time with Sebastion. At least the Thanksgiving holiday was coming up, so they'd have four whole days together.

"Feeling better, sweetie?" she asked.

He shrugged his little shoulders, put down the Pop-Tart, and leaned his head back against the booster seat.

She had missed drop-off and had to park and walk him in. His pre-K teacher, Penelope Watson, gave Charlotte a withering look when she entered the classroom with Sebastion. She was a stickler for punctuality, and this wasn't the first time they'd been late.

"So sorry we're late. It's been a morning."

Sebastion wrapped his arms around Charlotte's leg. "I wanna go home."

Penelope knelt at eye level with him. "What's wrong, Sebastion? I thought you were excited to go to the Audubon Center today."

"Tummy hurts."

She stood and gave Charlotte a concerned look. "Is he sick?"

Charlotte leaned down and embraced Sebastion. "I need to talk to Ms. Watson for a moment. Go play, and I'll see you later."

He reluctantly walked into the classroom and joined some boys playing with cars.

"He's been a little needy lately. Things are a bit upside down at home. His doctor says it's a coping mechanism and not to coddle him. I'm sure he'll be his old self once you're on your way."

"It's going to be a long day. Are you sure he's up to it?"

"Yes, I know he'd regret missing it. Once I'm gone, he'll be fine."

Mrs. Watson arched a brow, then nodded. "Okay. I'll keep a close eye on him."

"Thanks." She looked over and saw Sebastion laughing with another boy. Relieved, she slid from the classroom and took off for work.

The morning flew, and she didn't have time to give Sebastion another thought as she made her ad presentation. When she returned to her office, she was alarmed to see that she had four missed calls from his school but no messages. She dialed the school's number from her office phone with a shaking hand. When she gave the receptionist her name, she was put on hold and transferred. Finally, the headmaster's voice came over the line.

"Mrs. Fleming?"

Her hold on the phone tightened. "Yes?"

There was a pause and then, "I'm very sorry to inform you that there's been an accident."

The blood began pounding in her ears, and she couldn't get a deep breath.

"Is Sebastion okay?"

"There's no easy way to say this. The bus he was on collided with a truck and went over the Chesapeake Bay Bridge. I'm afraid there were no survivors."

PART ONE
CHARLOTTE

CHAPTER
ONE

10 Months Later

Charlotte shielded her eyes from the harsh sunlight with her pillow. "Eli, what the hell?" She was still half asleep but thoroughly irritated.

"It's almost noon, Charlotte. We need to talk. I can't live like this anymore."

"It's Saturday. What's the big deal?" she said.

"I'm dropping Harper off at the mall with her friends. I'll be back in half an hour. Please make sure that you're up." He slammed the bedroom door as he left.

She'd been in bed for almost twelve hours, yet she was still exhausted. She was always exhausted. Pushing herself to a sitting position, she forced herself to get up, shuffled to the bathroom, and turned the shower on. The last thing she wanted was to have another argument with Eli. She already knew she was being a shit mother to Harper and an even worse wife to him. But he wasn't the one who sent their four-year-old son to his death because of a fucking meeting. Of course, she wouldn't have had to if Eli's mistake hadn't forced her to return to work full-time. The only person she hated more than herself was him. She grabbed the prescription bottle from the counter and downed a pill, cupping her hand under the bathroom faucet to wash it down. Moving toward the shower, she put her hand in to test the water, then stepped inside and closed her eyes as the hot water beat down upon her.

When she finished, she threw her wet hair into a clip and put on sweats and a T-shirt. Most of her clothes hung on her these days. She was slim to begin with, and the extra twenty pounds she'd lost in the past year gave her a gaunt, haunted look. But what difference did it make? She rarely left the house anymore. She sighed when she heard the sound of Eli's car pulling into the garage. She opened the bedroom door and walked downstairs to the kitchen. Time to face the music.

"Glad you're up. Can I make you a coffee or tea?" he asked.

Charlotte nodded. "Coffee, thanks."

She observed him as he put the pod into the coffee maker, grabbed her mug, and added some creamer. These days she felt more like a spectator than a participant in her life, as if she were floating outside of herself. He put the mug down in front of her then took a seat and tented his hands. Clearing his throat a few times, he finally spoke.

"This is really hard for me to say, Char, but if you don't make some changes, I don't think I can keep going."

Heat rushed to her face, and her mouth fell open. "What are you saying?"

"Something's gotta give. It's been almost a year—"

She scoffed. "So what? I'm supposed to magically get over the fact that my four-year-old son died because the calendar says so? What is wrong with you?"

He stood up, pacing. "We're all grieving. I'll never get over losing Sebastion. But we have another child. I caught Harper drinking yesterday. Our thirteen-year-old, drunk! But why not?" His face was red now. "She has no mother to speak of. I can't do everything around here and be there for her too. You need to get into therapy, a grief group, or something. But either you rejoin the land of the living, or we'll need to take some time apart. And Harper will stay with me."

A part of her knew he was right. She hadn't been a mother to Harper since that horrible day. It wasn't like she hadn't tried. But every time she felt a glimmer of hope that maybe, just maybe, she could go on with her life, that voice inside reminded her that if she'd let Sebastion stay home that day, he'd still be alive. She had put her job before her son, and it cost her everything. How was she ever supposed to laugh again, to feel good, to enjoy life when she had been responsible for her son's death? For Harper's sake, she was glad that Eli had found the strength to function, but a part of her couldn't understand how he could so quickly resume his life. Whenever she heard him laughing or saw him doing something he enjoyed, it infuriated her. The urge to shake him and ask him how he could be so cold, so cavalier, burned inside her. But instead, she had disappeared inside of herself. She took a sip of her coffee and leveled a look at him.

"Fine. I'll start seeing Dr. Morrison again. But I want you to know that I will never forgive you for threatening me this way." She got up from the table and walked past him without another word.

CHAPTER
TWO

After two months of seeing Dr. Morrison, Charlotte grudgingly admitted that Eli had been right, even though she still resented his heavy-handedness. Her new meds were helping considerably. She was no longer comatose, moving through her day zombielike, and was starting to accomplish things. If she was honest with herself, she had to concede that accepting help was the only thing that had made her start trying again. She'd resumed taking Harper to school each day and forced herself to focus on her daughter when they were together. While she would never be the Charlotte she used to be, she was doing her best to be the mother that Harper deserved.

"Do you think you'll go back to work?" Harper asked as Charlotte drove.

She suddenly saw herself in her office, getting the terrible news. There was no way she could go back there. She shook her head. "No, that chapter of my life is over."

"Well, like, aren't you bored being home all day? You've got to do something, right? Madison says it's not good to have no purpose in life."

She bit back a sarcastic retort. Eli's assistant, Madison, had stepped in a lot over the past year, picking up Harper when Eli was tied up and Charlotte too depressed to leave the house. But she didn't like the idea of the woman talking about her, especially with her daughter.

"When did she say that?" she asked, keeping her voice even.

Harper shrugged. "A while ago. After you went back to the doctor, I think. She said something like it was good that you were getting some help and that it would be good for you to go back to work."

Now Charlotte was fuming. What the hell was Eli doing talking to his assistant about her? She didn't want Harper to see that she was upset by it, so she simply smiled.

"One step at a time, babe. I'm just getting my footing again. Although I might do some consulting. One of my former colleagues reached out. She's starting a social media business and asked if I'd be willing to work on a per-project basis."

Harper's blue eyes twinkled, and her face broke into a wide smile. "Mom, that's awesome. You should."

Maybe doing some consulting work *would* be a good distraction. A way to take her mind off the past. She'd text Patricia when she got home and tell her she'd give it a try. Nothing too arduous, a small job that would require only a few hours a week.

They pulled up to the school drop-off line, and Harper gathered her backpack and jumped out. "See ya."

Charlotte watched as Harper's shiny blond ponytail bobbed up and down as she ran toward her friends. Despite what had happened a few months ago with the drinking, Harper was an easy and happy child. She was popular and did well in school, her only failing being that she was too eager to please and, therefore, susceptible to peer pressure. They had grounded her for a month, and Harper swore that was the last time she'd drink alcohol. Charlotte wasn't naïve enough to believe that her daughter would never slip again, but she hoped for Harper's sake that she would stay on the straight and narrow.

She thought about Harper's question about being bored. The truth was, it took all her energy to get dressed, drive Harper to school, and take care of the necessities of their household. She still slept most of the day away and would set an alarm for when it was time to pick Harper up. Her depression wasn't gone, merely hibernating from pill to pill.

She contemplated doing a few errands, but only because she was stalling. Today was the day she'd promised Dr. Morrison that she'd pack up Sebastion's room, and she didn't feel ready to face it. But the reality was she would never be ready, so she drove straight home and marched into his room. She sat on his bed and brought his pillow to her nose, but it didn't smell like him anymore. Those first few weeks, she'd barely left his room, his teddy bear clutched in her arms as she cried herself to sleep in his bed. She looked around the room a final time. At the *Toy Story* wallpaper, the Hot Wheels cars lining his dresser, and the bookshelf holding his favorite books and stuffed animals. She closed her eyes, imagining for a moment that he'd be home soon, his little hand pushing the blond curls away from his eyes—cobalt-blue eyes that stole their color from the Caribbean. She picked up *Where the Wild Things Are* and clutched it to her chest, remembering the last time she'd read it to him and how he'd run around the room pretending to be one of the creatures from the book. A sob escaped her. She put the book down and ran from the room. She'd pack it up another day. She wasn't ready.

She flipped on the television and plopped down on the sofa. She'd doze until it was time to get Harper from school. Her phone buzzed as she was about to pull a blanket over her—a text from Eli.

Dinner tonight? I was thinking Dominic's.

She started to type back, then stopped. She wasn't in the mood to go out to dinner, but she *had* promised Eli she would make more effort. But she was still pissed about Madison's comments to Harper. She would talk to him about it at home tonight. She sighed. There had been a time when Eli was her entire world. Charlotte had been born into privilege, a third-generation member of the well-known Van Arsdale family. They'd been in Maryland since the 1800s, and her great-great-grandfather had invented the travel iron that was now in all the major hotel chains. Charlotte's parents were big believers in making your own way. They paid for her private schools, college, and her basic necessities. But they refused to give her a trust fund. She would inherit their money someday but it wasn't something she counted on. She had always had a job from the time she was a teenager, and after college, she went into advertising, where she worked hard and was promoted often.

When she met Eli, he was an up-and-comer at a prominent investment firm in downtown Baltimore. He came from a more modest background, and she felt sure when she introduced him to her parents, they would appreciate his work ethic and fall in love with him as she had. But they had disapproved. The things that she loved about him—his spontaneity, sense of adventure, and passion for living—they saw as unstable, reckless, and undignified. But when they realized there was no dissuading her, they gave her the wedding she'd always dreamed of. And when Harper, her honeymoon baby, was born, they embraced Eli with open arms, so enamored were they of their grandchild.

During those first few years, they were both rising stars in their chosen fields and their marriage thrived. Staring at his text, she recalled the day they'd looked at the house they lived in now. It wasn't on the real estate agent's list because it was way above their price range, but Charlotte had noticed the open house sign when they pulled onto the street to look at a different house.

"Let's just take a look," she'd said to Eli, and he'd smiled and agreed.

Charlotte hadn't believed in love at first sight until she stepped into that house. From the moment she set eyes on it, she was besotted. It was a white colonial that overlooked a large creek. The view from the bay window in the kitchen was spectacular; it revealed a rolling green lawn that led to a large dock on the water. Beautiful sailboats dotted the creek, and she felt like she could sit there and watch the sun spray diamonds over the water for hours. The kitchen was a dream too, with butter-yellow cabinets, top-of-the-line appliances, and a gorgeous custom-built island that could accommodate twelve. She could picture them having dinner here, then going on the boat that they'd have to buy. She would plant hydrangeas in all colors and teach Harper how to garden. They would fill the rooms with more children, laughter, and love, and it would be perfect.

They both had been quiet as they walked through, and Charlotte's heart sank as they left, knowing it was above their means and that everything else they looked at would pale in comparison.

Eli kept watching her face, reading her mind despite her best attempts at appearing blasé. "It's your dream house, isn't it?"

"It's beautiful, but it's too much. One day."

They spent the rest of the afternoon looking at other houses, but her heart wasn't in it. "Maybe we should just wait," she told him. "Rent a while longer."

"Whatever you want, babe," was all he said.

She had put the idea of moving out of her head. A month later, on a Saturday, he suggested taking Harper to the park. It wasn't until they drove past it that she realized something was up. "You missed the entrance," she said.

He looked over at her with a mischievous grin. "I just have a quick stop to make."

When they'd pulled onto the street, she couldn't contain her curiosity any longer. "What are we doing here?"

"Patience," he teased.

Her heart beat faster when he pulled into the driveway of the house she'd fallen in love with. "Why . . ."

He got out of the car and opened her door. "Welcome home, Mrs. Fleming."

Grand gestures were a part of Eli's makeup and she loved him for it. He was always doing things to make her happy. And not just the big stuff. Whether it was a book she mentioned or a scarf she admired in a store window, he remembered and would surprise her with it. But this was over the top.

"I thought we couldn't afford it!"

"It's all taken care of—my bonus. I put a huge down payment on it. The mortgage payments will be more than manageable."

And his bonuses were more than enough . . . for a while. She should have known the returns Eli made for them and his clients were too good to be true. Everything came crashing down when Sebastion turned four. The SEC closed down the firm, and the CEO and CFO, and a handful of other executives, went to prison. Eli swore he knew nothing about the illegal activities and was never arrested. Charlotte believed in his innocence, but it didn't make the situation any easier. Some part of her found it hard to believe he hadn't known. He was an intelligent man; how could he not discern what was happening? Even though he was cleared, he couldn't overcome the stigma his tenure there had stained him with. His clients lost millions, and he became a pariah in the industry. That was when she had to return to work, all leading to that fateful day and an ignored tummy ache.

She started typing again.

Let's plan something for the weekend. I'm beat.

He'd be disappointed, but it was better than getting into an argument in public.

CHAPTER
THREE

She waited until Harper had gone to sleep before confronting Eli. He was watching a show when she walked into the living room.

"Mind pausing that a minute? I need to talk to you."

He grabbed the remote and did so, then looked over at her. "What's up."

She took a seat on the sofa. "Harper said something today that concerns me."

"What did she say?"

"Apparently, Madison thinks it's appropriate to discuss my mental state with our daughter."

"What?"

"She told Harper that it was good that I was getting help, and that I should go back to work so I have a purpose in life."

"I don't know what to say. Are you sure Harper got that right?"

"Why are you discussing me with your assistant? It's none of her business what I do."

He put both hands up. "Okay, look. She was out of line talking to Harper, I'll admit that. But you can't have it both ways, Char. When you took to your bed all those months, who do you think pitched in to help? It's only been a couple of months since you've been up and around. All I did was let her know I didn't need her help anymore because you were better."

Charlotte deflated. He was right. Like it or not, Madison had been there for their family. At the time, she was too numb to care. But she cared now, and she wanted Madison out of their business.

"You're right, she has been helpful. But it was inappropriate for her to talk about me to Harper. I don't want her in our personal business."

"Of course. Don't worry."

"But I do worry. I think we've crossed a line. In retrospect, we should have made some other kind of arrangement. And I know I let everything fall on you. But I don't like that your assistant has been privy to our private life."

He sighed. "It's no secret that we've been through hell. No one is judging you for—"

"Who said anything about judging me?"

"Don't twist my words. All I'm saying is that it's public knowledge what we all went through. I went to some of those support groups with the other families. Everyone has handled this in their own way, and it's been life altering. So, yeah, in normal circumstances, I'd keep my work and personal life separate. But in this case, it was unavoidable."

She could never bring herself to go to those groups. Sharing her grief felt like diluting it. She didn't want to commiserate with the other parents about what they'd lost. Her grief was all she had. It was hers and hers alone, all she had left of Sebastion. Eli was right. Everyone did grieve in their own way. "I see your point. But please talk with her and redefine the boundaries."

He nodded. "I will."

She let the subject drop despite still wondering how much Eli had depended on Madison emotionally. She couldn't help but think about what else Eli had been discussing with Madison. Could anything be going on between the two of them? Were his late nights at the office comprised of more than work?

Madison had worked for Eli at his old company. He hadn't started his new job until after the accident, so Charlotte had been too shattered to pay much attention. But thinking about it now, it struck her as strange that Eli had hired Madison to work for him at his new firm a year later. Surely she'd already gotten another job.

She had met Madison at Eli's previous company's Christmas party four years ago. Madison sauntered up to Charlotte and Eli with a broad smile on her pretty face, her long, dark hair reaching the middle of her back. The red silk dress she wore accentuated her curves in all the right places. "Stunning" was the word that came to Charlotte's mind. Eli introduced the two of them, and to Charlotte's surprise, the woman pulled her into a hug.

"I feel like I already know you. Eli talks about you all the time," she'd gushed.

Charlotte gave her a stiff smile. "So nice to meet you, Madison."

"My gosh. Your pictures don't do you justice. Has anyone ever told you that you look just like Charlize Theron?"

People had. "That's nice of you to say."

"Well, enjoy the party." She'd given Eli a long look before walking away. At the time, Charlotte had been slightly disquieted, but Eli had never given her a reason to doubt him. Over the years, Charlotte learned that Madison could be intrusive and overly friendly, but left it at that. Now, her suspicions surfaced. Charlotte hadn't been much of a wife to Eli this past year, and even though no one in their right mind could blame Charlotte for how the tragedy had affected her, the reality was that Eli was vulnerable. Had Madison taken advantage of that vulnerability?

If Charlotte wanted to save her marriage, it was time to open her heart to her husband again. But try as she might, finding that feeling of tenderness and attraction she'd once had was as difficult to recapture as trying to hold quicksilver in your hand.

CHAPTER
FOUR

Are we ever going to have sex again?" Eli asked after Charlotte rolled away from him.

A knot of dread wound itself in the pit of her stomach. Since their conversation about Madison last week, she'd been doing her best to be more affectionate, but her desire for sex was nonexistent. She reluctantly turned toward him. "Those are not exactly words to put me in the mood," she joked weakly, but she felt guilty when she saw the hurt look on his face. "I'm sorry. I'm just not myself. I'm trying."

He nodded. "Yeah, I know. I'm sorry too. It's just that I miss you."

"I miss you too," she answered automatically, although it wasn't true. She didn't know if her desire for him would ever return, but she couldn't tell him that. She'd asked her therapist if her marriage would ever recover. Dr. Morrison told her that if they could ride this storm out, she might find that her marriage would emerge even stronger. In the meantime, she just had to stall. "Dr. Morrison said the anti-depressants can diminish sex drive too. But I don't think I should stop the medicine since it's helping me to function better."

He shook his head. "No, no. It's fine. Your well-being is the most important thing right now."

"Speaking of my well-being . . . Remember Patricia from my job?"

"I think so."

"She started her own marketing company and wants to hire me on a project-by-project basis to do some social media. What do you think?"

His eyes lit up. "Char, I think that's a great idea. What do *you* think?"

"As long as it's not too demanding, I think it might be good for me to have something new to focus on."

"I think so too."

"Okay, I'll call her tomorrow. Night." She closed her eyes, clutching the pillow to her chest, and tried to empty her mind. Since she'd weaned herself from the sleeping pills, her nights had become restless. Calming thoughts, she reminded herself, but her brain didn't listen. Unbidden, the image came again. The one her mind had made up of the bus careening off the bridge into the icy waters of the Chesapeake Bay. She imagined the screams and looks of terror on the children's faces and then her sweet Sebastion, sinking, sinking until he was beyond rescue. Her heart was hammering in her chest, and she jumped up from the bed.

"You okay?" Eli mumbled, half asleep.

"Yeah," she lied. "Just can't sleep. Going to read in the other room for a bit."

She grabbed her robe from the back of the bathroom door and slipped from the room. Her breath came in uneven gasps as she ran into the living room and sat down. Putting her head between her knees, she practiced the breathing technique Dr. Morrison had taught her until her breath returned to normal. Would this torment ever end? She flipped the television on and pulled a blanket over her shivering body. She forced herself to focus on the movie she'd seen many times before until, finally, her lids became heavy, and she surrendered to the blessed escape of sleep.

A gentle nudge on her shoulder made her open her eyes. Sunlight streamed into the room.

"Rough night?" Eli asked, a look of concern on his face.

She sat up and rubbed her eyes. "Didn't mean to sleep here. Guess I dozed off."

"I made a pot of coffee. I'll take Harper this morning. She's already in the car. I didn't want to wake you."

"Thanks." She got up, walked into the kitchen, and poured herself a cup.

Eli leaned down to kiss her. "Have a good day. Let me know how it goes with Patricia."

She nodded. Before she lost her nerve, she went into the bedroom, got her phone, and fired off a text to Patricia to let her know she was interested. Not five minutes later, her phone rang.

"Well, that was fast," she said, laughing.

"You made my day," Patricia answered. "I've been on pins and needles, hoping you'd say yes."

"Don't get too excited. I'm dipping my toe back in. I'm not ready to go full throttle."

"I know, sweetie. How are you? Really?"

Charlotte sighed. "Shitty. But less shitty than I was two months ago."

"I guess that's something. I won't try to pretend to understand. I know it's something you never get over. I just want you to know that I'm always here for you if you want to talk about Sebastion."

Hearing his name was so refreshing. Everyone tiptoed around it. As if by not mentioning his name, Charlotte could forget the pain. But they didn't understand that she didn't want to forget. It was like losing him all over again. She wanted to talk about him, to remember him and the joy he'd brought to her life. "Thank you. You're right. I'll never get over it, but I'm trying to regain some semblance of a life. At least for Harper's sake."

"For your sake too, honey. You deserve it."

But that was just it. She didn't deserve it, and no one would ever convince her that she did. She didn't want to hear worthless platitudes about how she should handle her grief. But at least Patricia was trying. "I tried to pack up his room yesterday. I couldn't do it. My therapist is pushing me, but it seems disloyal. Like I'm trying to forget him."

"You go at your own pace. I don't care what your therapist says. You'll know when you're ready."

"Thanks, I appreciate that. Okay, enough about me. Tell me about this project."

Patricia filled her in on the client she'd be working with. "They do custom book merch. They've been on Facebook, and I want them on Instagram too. You know, lots of authors there. You've got tons of experience with both, and they have a decent Facebook following, so they want to keep doing some ads and giveaways there. I'd also like you to create reels and grow their following on Insta. I'll set up a Zoom to introduce you."

"Sure, that sounds fine. I'll check out their website and current stats and develop a proposal. What's their budget?"

"Decent. I'll email all the details and send over some times for the Zoom. Sound good?"

"Yep. Thanks."

Charlotte felt a tiny spark of excitement. She was looking forward to the research and analytics that came with a project like this. After pouring another cup of coffee, she went to the room that used to be her home office. Everything looked the same. The only reason it wasn't dust-covered was thanks to Enid, who came twice a week to clean the house. She opened the laptop and plugged in the charger. This was good. Exactly what she needed. She returned to the bedroom to shower and get dressed. She might even have a little breakfast before she got started.

CHAPTER
FIVE

Charlotte hadn't been on social media since Sebastion died. She'd deactivated all her accounts, unable to bear the messages of sympathy and, even worse, the trolls who made hurtful comments about the accident being a hoax. Now that she was going to be managing the social media accounts for Book Brag, it was time she plunged back in so she could see what had changed. She opened a new Facebook account, sending friend requests to close friends and liking pages similar to Book Brag's. She did the same with Instagram and TikTok and began to follow accounts that followed them. Not much had changed on Facebook, but Instagram reels had become more popular than static posts. She was surprised when two hours passed while she watched reel after reel. No wonder it was referred to as a rabbit hole. She couldn't deny the appeal of the rapid-fire promotions, catchy music, and colorful graphics. She had a lot of catching up to do. It suddenly occurred to her that rather than offering her the job because of her skills, Patricia might be trying to help her return to the land of the living. She sighed. She'd do her best not to let her friend down. She navigated to a search bar, looked up articles on current trends, and made a list of influencers and bookmarked videos to watch later. She'd promised Patricia that she'd have a proposal ready in two weeks. Now she wondered if that timing was too aggressive.

It was time to pick up Harper, and as she drove, she formulated her plan of attack. Spending the next three days reading and watching videos would give her a solid enough foundation to begin. Then she'd analyze Book Brag's top three competitors and compare their websites, followers, posts, and marketing campaigns. After that, she'd be ready to put together her proposal. Her mind was already exploding with ideas, and she felt alive for the first time since that horrible day. She had a smile on her face when Harper slid into the front seat. Her daughter's face broke out into a grin.

"You look happy," Harper said.

"I had a good day. How about you? School good?"

Harper shrugged. "School's school. But I did get invited to Farrah's slumber party, so that's awesome."

"Oh, honey, that's great. When is it?"

"This Saturday. I have to make sure my present is really cool."

"Okay, we'll go shopping tomorrow."

"Um, Mom, I was wondering . . ."

"What?"

"Well, my birthday's next month, and, um, I don't want my friends to see Sebastion's room with all his stuff in there."

Charlotte stiffened. "Why? What does that have to do with your friends?"

"Like, don't get mad, but Hayden was over the other day, and she went in. She said it's morbid. Like a shrine or something."

The heat rose to Charlotte's face. "I don't want your friends going in there. Do you understand? And you can tell Hayden that it's none of her fucking business." She couldn't stop the words from flying from her mouth. She never used profanity in front of Harper. But she was furious at the thought of anyone going through her son's things.

"Mom!"

"I'm sorry. But Hayden had no right to go in there."

Harper didn't answer, and when she glanced over, Charlotte saw that she was crying.

"Harper . . ."

"I miss him too, you know. You're not the only one."

Charlotte reached out to pat her hand, but Harper snatched it back. "I know you do. I'm sorry if seeing his room still there makes you uncomfortable, but can you understand? I'm not ready."

"Whatever."

They rode in silence the rest of the way home, Charlotte's short-lived feeling of well-being completely gone. She couldn't seem to do anything right anymore. She pulled into the driveway, and Harper bolted from the car and went into the house. Charlotte rested her head on the steering wheel, breathing deeply, telling herself it would all be okay. At times like these, she wondered if her family would be better off without her. Eli could find some nice woman to marry who would give Harper the attention she deserved. Bake cookies with her, take an interest in her hobbies, and do more than pay lip service half-distracted. "Don't be stupid," she said out loud. Tomorrow. She'd pack up the room tomorrow. It was the least she could do for her only remaining child.

The next day, still thinking about her conversation with Harper, she stopped at the grocery store. She'd bake chocolate chip cookies. They were Harper's favorite. When was the last time she'd baked anything? She walked down the baking aisle and grabbed flour, baking powder, and chips. As she was about to push the cart forward, she looked up and froze. Her heart began to pound furiously. She dropped the bag of chocolate chips in her hand and ran toward the little boy at the end of the aisle. It was Sebastion! She touched his shoulder and he turned around.

"Can I help you?" A woman ran up to her.

Charlotte swallowed the lump in her throat. Of course it wasn't him. "I'm sorry. I thought your son was someone else. I apologize." She backed away. The woman was still looking at her with suspicion. Then the tears came, and she ran from the store, leaving her cart in the middle of the aisle. It was happening again. Just when she began to feel somewhat normal, her mind played tricks on her. Would it ever end?

CHAPTER
SIX

She got as far as taking down the posters on the wall. But when she went to the closet and pulled one of Sebastion's sweaters down, she began to cry uncontrollably. Eli had offered to do it with her, but she needed to go at her own pace and sort through things herself. He would just pack it all up efficiently and she couldn't bear that. She sat down on the bed and looked around the room. It felt wrong to dismantle it. This was too hard. She couldn't do it. So instead, she drove to the hardware store, bought a deadbolt lock, watched a video on YouTube on how to install it, and did so. She'd always been technically inclined, much more so than Eli, who couldn't hammer a nail properly. She felt a sense of accomplishment when she put the key in and locked the door. Problem solved. Now none of Harper's friends would go in there.

She was behind on her research, so she went into the office with a strong cup of coffee and opened her laptop. Navigating to Facebook, she saw that she had some friend requests from old colleagues and high school and college friends. She accepted them and spent some time looking at their pages. Then she remembered the other reason she'd gotten off social media. Everyone seemed so happy and complete. Beautiful pictures of family holidays, babies being born, vacations. It made her loss feel even larger. Sighing, she shut the laptop and leaned back in her chair, summoning the memory of their last family vacation.

They'd gone to Rehoboth Beach the last week of summer. Every year, they rented the same house right on the beach. Charlotte loved sleeping with the sliding doors open and listening to the crashing waves. Both Harper and Sebastion loved the beach, and they'd spend all day building sandcastles and playing in the surf. Harper had brought a friend with her, and the two girls walked the beach every day, shyly smiling at cute boys, trying to act older than their twelve years. Sebastion, only four, was happy digging in the sand and playing in the small wading pool Eli would bring down every morning and filled with ocean water. It was simple and wholesome, and Eli insisted she take some time to read her book while he watched over Sebastion. He was great in that way, so unlike many of her friends' husbands, who believed childcare was the mother's responsibility. Her friends always came back from their vacations needing a vacation. But she and Eli had worked out a rhythm and balance that gave them each time to relax. Sebastion had been delighted when his digging yielded sand crabs, and he'd run over to her, excited.

"Mommy, Mommy, crabbies. Can we cook them?"

She laughed. Even at his young age, he was a true Marylander who'd had his first taste of steamed blue crab at age two.

"No, sweetie, those are different kinds of crab."

"Oh, I'll put it back."

They'd had their photo taken by the young guy selling telescope photos. It was the last picture ever taken of the four of them.

She stood up and stretched, pacing briefly to try to center herself. She needed to focus. She watched two more videos on social media trends then picked up her phone and opened Instagram. She was following a little over four hundred accounts right now—a mix of authors, bookstores, and publishers, to get a sense of what the ads targeted to that segment looked like. She scrolled through posts of book covers, writing advice, television series, quotes, and more books. She liked the book-related posts to see how that would affect the algorithm and narrow down the sponsored content she saw. After an hour, her eyes began to blur as she clicked on a story from a bookstore in Florida. Her heart sped up, and it took her a minute to absorb what she was seeing. She scrolled back down and stared. A group of kids sat in a circle, being read to by someone in a Cat in the Hat costume. Her eyes rested on a little boy half turned away. Could it be?

She took a screenshot and enlarged the photo. It looked exactly like Sebastion. His hair was shorter and his face thinner, but otherwise he was a dead ringer for her son. But of course, this wasn't the first time she thought she saw him. It seemed like she saw him everywhere. She'd been told that was common. She studied the picture again. A surge of hope soared through her. They had never found some of the children's bodies, Sebastion's among them. Had he somehow survived the crash? The boy in the picture was wearing shorts and a T-shirt she'd never seen. She zoomed in farther and that's when she noticed the strawberry birthmark above his knee. At least, she thought that's what it was. Enlarging it made it a little bit blurry. Yes, she was sure, it was the same shape as the one on Sebastion's leg! It *was* him—a little older, but undeniably her Sebastion. She broke out into a cold sweat. Grabbing a pad of paper and a pen, she clicked on the account's profile. The Sunshine Bookstore in Rosemont, Florida. It looked like a small independent bookstore. There was a username on the bottom of the photo; @rebeccabronson had tagged the bookstore. She opened the laptop, found the bookstore's website, and dialed the number.

"It's a beautiful day at Sunshine Books."

"Hello, yes, may I speak with your social media person?"

"That would be me. Social media person, manager, owner. How can I help you?"

"Well, this may sound crazy, but I just saw the picture on your website and I was hoping you could tell me when it was taken." Charlotte didn't know why, but something kept her from disclosing the truth.

"Which picture?"

"The children being read to by the Cat in the Hat."

"I'm sorry, who is this?"

"My name is Charlotte Fleming, and my son has been missing for a year. He was in that photo."

"Oh my gosh, that's horrible. It was a birthday party last week. I don't feel comfortable giving out the name of the person who booked it, but if you call the police, I'd be happy to release the information to them. You understand, I have to be careful these days."

Charlotte resisted the urge to press, realizing it might do more than good. "Okay, I understand. Of course. The police."

She hung up, still reeling. She called Eli.

"You need to come home. Something's happened."

"What? Are you okay?"

Suddenly, she couldn't catch her breath again. "It's Sebastion. I think he's alive! I saw his picture. I'm going to call the police." She filled him in on everything she'd just discovered.

"Whoa, whoa. Hold on. I'm coming home right now. Don't call anyone."

She heard the skepticism in his voice. "I'm not imagining this, Eli. It's him!"

"Okay, okay, just wait until I get there. Let's take this one step at a time. I'm leaving now. Wait for me."

Charlotte wanted to jump out of her skin. She looked at the screenshot she'd taken and went to the profile of the person who'd tagged the bookstore. Shit. It was a private Instagram account. She clicked the follow button and hoped the woman would click accept. It took all the restraint she could muster not to book a flight to Florida. She went to Facebook and typed in the woman's name. She had a Facebook profile. She went to the Messenger app and began to type:

You don't know me, but my son went missing a year ago. I have reason to believe that he was at a birthday party at Sunshine Bookstore. Can you please contact me? Whoever has him has kidnapped him. I am desperate. I'm attaching a picture here of my son, Sebastion.

Charlotte sent a picture of herself with Sebastion taken a few weeks before the accident and included her cell phone number. Hopefully, the woman would get back to her. Another thought occurred to her. And she froze. What if the woman she'd just sent a message to was the one who had taken Sebastion, and she'd just tipped her off? She needed to slow down and think this through before making any more rash moves. She'd wait to go to the police until she had more information. The last thing she needed was for them to dismiss her as a grieving mother with no hold on reality. She would go back over every detail of that day with clear eyes. Somehow, her son had escaped that terrible fate. She was going to find out how. She got up and walked down the hall. She unlocked the door to Sebastion's room and looked around with eyes of hope. Now she understood why she'd never been able to put his things away. She was going to bring him home.

CHAPTER
SEVEN

She was already waiting in the kitchen when she heard Eli's car pull into the garage. He ran inside and held out his hand. "Let me see the picture."

She gave him her phone with the picture enlarged on the screen. "See. He's right there in the green T-shirt."

He stared at the screen for a long moment then looked at her with pity. "I'll admit he looks like Sebastion, but the picture's a bit blurry. I'm sorry, Char. I think it's just a child who resembles him."

She shook her head. "No, you're wrong. How can you not see that this is him? Look at his leg." She pointed. "The birthmark! It's him. I know it's him."

"It's not a clear picture, Char." He sighed. "Let's sit," he said, guiding her to the chairs at the kitchen table. "Honey, you know what they said. The bus sank into the Chesapeake Bay. By the time they reached the bus it was too late, they had all drowned. There's no way that Sebastion can be alive."

She gave him a cold look. "I'm perfectly aware of the details of the accident. But I know my son. And that's him in that picture. Nothing you say will change my mind. I'm going to the police tomorrow and showing them this picture. Then the bookstore will have to release the name of the woman who booked the party. I'm going to find him."

"Be reasonable. All you're going to do is make the insurance company dispute the claim. And for what? To chase down some child that looks like ours? I wish he were alive too. Don't you think I wish there were some way this was all one big mistake? But it's not. This is only going to set you back."

"The insurance? Are you for real? I still don't understand why you took out a hundred-thousand-dollar policy on our child!"

"It's whole life, and I have policies for both Harper and Sebastion. It's good financial planning. Don't you remember, we talked about this." He shook his head. "It would have been a nice nest egg for Sebastion when he grew up." His voice caught. "I never thought . . ."

"Well, I don't care if the insurance company tries to take it back. How can you even bring that up?"

He sighed. "Charlotte, you know our financial situation is still precarious. I used that money to pay the mortgage payments that were in arrears and the credit card debt we accrued before I went back to work. All I'm saying is, why raise a red flag? As hard as it is to accept, Sebastion is gone. If you try to reopen the case, they could make us pay that back. We're not in a position to do that."

She gave him an incredulous look. "The hell with the money. I'm going to find our son. I can't even believe—"

"Charlotte, I've been a patient man. I've been both mother and father to Harper while you've slept the better part of a year away." He put his hand up. "Not that I'm blaming you. But now that you are finally functioning again, you're chasing ghosts. That picture proves nothing. It's not Sebastion. You have to face the cold reality that he's gone. The first responders found the bus. It was underwater. There's no way he survived that."

She shook her head. "You don't know that for sure since they didn't find his body."

"Remember what the report said. The bus driver wasn't found, nor were some of the other children. He must have tried to help them get out, and they drifted off. Bodies are lost in the water every day. What do you think? Magically, a helicopter that no one saw came and pulled him out? It's crazy."

But she knew in her bones that her son was alive. This wasn't like the other times. "I don't know how, but somehow, he escaped. We're missing something. I'm requesting a copy of the accident report. I need to see who they identified and who they didn't. Our son is out there somewhere, and I'm going to find him."

CHAPTER
EIGHT

Eli hadn't even said goodbye when he left for work the next day. After dropping Harper at school, Charlotte had headed straight to the Maryland Transportation Authority to request an official copy of the police report from the accident. She took a deep breath now, her hand resting on the sealed envelope, trying to muster the strength to read it. What if Eli was right? If her son really was dead, did she want to add to her grief by reading a vivid description of everything that had happened that day? She shook her head as if to empty it of her doubts and ripped the envelope open. Her heart sped up as she pulled the thick document from the envelope and read the title: School Bus Run-Off Bridge Accident, Annapolis, Maryland. She moved to the table of contents and was stunned to see that the report was eighty-five pages long. With a sinking heart, she read the first page, containing the narrative describing the accident. Seeing it all in black and white made it all the more real, and she couldn't stop herself from imagining what it must have been like inside that bus. She flashed back to that morning, wishing with all her heart that she'd let her son stay home that day.

Her eyes moved to the narrative of the pre-accident events, which detailed the field trip that was supposed to have taken place. The last stop the bus made before the accident was at McDonald's. Witnesses reported seeing it pull in at 10:00 a.m. and not leaving for almost half an hour. That was strange. Why would they stop at a restaurant so soon after leaving school, and why for so long?

She studied the page with the medical and pathological information. It had a diagram of the bus, and a legend at the bottom explained the designation next to each seat with the injury level. They were all F for fatal, with the exception of five seats—the ones of the bodies that were never found. The bus driver's seat was also empty. She knew that the bus was filled because a friend of Sebastion's turned his permission slip in too late, and there was no room left on the bus. She skimmed through the information on the bus driver's background as well as the description of the bus. It was all becoming too much for her. She flipped the pages until she reached the conclusion page. She already knew some of it because the driver was determined not to be at fault. Parents had wanted to sue the school, but the blame lay squarely on the driver of the truck that had hit them, and that driver had also perished. She leaned back in her chair and sighed. She needed to look over the list of names of the bodies that had been recovered. At the time, the only thing she'd cared about was that Sebastion's body hadn't been found.

She retrieved her file on the accident and pulled out the police report. Looking over the names, she realized that Sebastion's teacher, Penelope, wasn't listed as one of the bodies on the bus either. That seemed strange. She couldn't imagine that Penelope would have left any of the children. Aside from the bus driver, she was the only adult not accounted for. Charlotte could understand the bus driver, he was probably at the door trying to get the children out, but a teacher would be one of the last off the bus. And Penelope always struck Charlotte as a good teacher. There were times that she almost resented how close she was to Sebastion. Times the teacher would try to give Charlotte advice on ways to coax him out of a sullen mood or suggestions about what kinds of shows he might enjoy, as if she knew Charlotte's son better than Charlotte did.

Something was niggling at her. What was it? Something about Penelope. She went into her office and logged in to her mobile carrier. Navigating to last November's bill, she pulled up the phone log for that day. There it was. At the time, it hadn't registered with the shock of the accident. Before the missed calls from the school, which had come at 12:30 p.m., there was a missed call from Penelope's cell phone at 10:25 a.m. Why had Penelope called her? She navigated to the details for Eli's phone and saw that he also had a call from Penelope, but that call had lasted eleven seconds. Had he spoken to her? And if so, why hadn't he mentioned it? Penelope called them *before* the bus crashed, and around the same time they were at McDonald's. It had to have had something to do with Sebastion. Had he gotten lost in the crowd? That could be why they were there for so long. But surely, they wouldn't have left without finding him. His stomachache—maybe it had gotten worse. What if he'd gotten really sick, and the bus had dropped him and Penelope off at a hospital or medical center? Now she wondered if the reason their bodies were never found was because they weren't on the bus when it crashed! A surge of adrenaline rushed through her. That had to be the answer. But where were they now?

CHAPTER
NINE

Charlotte had been on the phone all afternoon. First to check each of the area's urgent care facilities and local hospitals to see if anyone matching Sebastion's description had come in that day. His name wasn't on any of their computers, and no one remembered seeing him. She also had them check under Penelope's name, but nothing. Next, she'd called the school to find out who Penelope's next of kin was, but they said that would violate their privacy policy. She opened her laptop to the memorial page the school had set up after the tragedy. Her heart skipped a beat when she saw Sebastion's picture, and a sob escaped her. Taking a deep breath, she scrolled down to the comments made by family members and friends. There were hundreds of messages, and it was tough going, but she had to see if anyone had left a message about Penelope Watson. An hour later, she finally found something.

To my wonderful sister, I'll carry you in my heart forever. Nora

She did a browser search for Nora Watson, but there were too many. She narrowed it down to Maryland and began meticulously looking at each one. Penelope had been in her twenties, so her sister would likely be close to her age. After another hour, no further ahead, she got up and made herself a cup of tea. It was like looking for a needle in a haystack. Social media might yield something. She returned to her office and went to Facebook to see if Penelope had a page. No luck. Then she searched Nora Watson and began to sort through the profiles. None of them seemed right. Frustrated, she glanced at her watch—almost seven. Harper would be home from her soccer game soon. She was surprised that Eli wasn't home yet. She picked up her cell phone and realized it was in silent mode. He had texted a while ago.

Last minute change of plans with a client. Taking them to dinner. Don't wait up.

Working late? She wondered again if something was going on with him and Madison. She would bring it up to her therapist. She was tempted to keep going with her internet sleuthing, but she knew Harper would be starving when she came in, and Charlotte suddenly felt guilty that she hadn't prepared anything for dinner. She went into the kitchen, opened the freezer, and pulled out a pizza. That would have to do.

Moments later, the front door opened, and Harper's footsteps echoed from the hallway.

"Mom, we won!"

She burst into the kitchen, all smiles, and Charlotte walked over to give her a hug. "Congrats, honey! That's great."

"I scored the winning goal. Everyone was cheering. I wish it had been a home game so you could have been there."

"Me too." The truth was that Charlotte could have chosen to drive the ninety minutes to the game; some of the other parents did, but she couldn't focus on anything other than whether her son was alive. At Eli's insistence, she hadn't told Harper anything, although she was bursting to. She could use an ally, but Eli was right; Harper needed to be kept in the dark until she had some answers. It wasn't fair to get her hopes up.

"I put a pepperoni pizza in for you," Charlotte told her.

"Cool. I'm gonna shower. Wanna watch an episode of *Grey's* with me?"

What she really wanted was to keep going with her search for Penelope's sister, but she nodded. "Love to."

"'Kay. I'll be back in a flash."

Charlotte pulled the pizza from the oven and cut it, then grabbed plates and sodas. Harper was back, a towel around her neck, her hair still wet from the shower, wearing her pajamas. Charlotte felt a tug in her heart. Harper was still so young, yet she'd grown so much over the past year. A deep feeling of regret washed over her, thinking about how much of her daughter's life she'd missed while she was buried in grief. No more. No matter what, she had to keep a balance. She would leave no stone unturned in investigating what she now believed was her son's disappearance rather than his death. But she had to make sure that she didn't neglect Harper in doing so. She would spend her days searching for answers, but her evenings would be reserved for her daughter. *What about your husband*, a little voice asked. She didn't have an answer.

CHAPTER
TEN

The following day, Charlotte was back at it, methodically going through the profile of every Nora Watson on Facebook. Some profiles had more public information available than others, and she narrowed it down to three women who might be related to Penelope. If only she had access to all their photos, she could see if there were any older ones of Penelope. Maybe Nora was married and her profile was under her married name, which Charlotte didn't have. She debated sending them all friend requests then thought better of it. Even if she found Penelope's sister, who knew if she could be trusted?

Next, she went to search the death records in Maryland to see if Penelope was listed. Eli and she had had to request a death certificate for the insurance company, and one was provided pretty quickly after the investigation when it became clear that there were no survivors. Navigating to the vital records website, she initiated a search for Penelope Watson's death certificate. It took her to an online order link. She typed in the information, but when she reached the end, she found that only the decedent's mother, father, spouse, or child could order a copy.

She picked up her phone and called the school. "Hi, Misty. It's Charlotte Fleming. How are you?"

"Oh, hi, Charlotte. It's nice to hear your voice. What can I do for you?"

Charlotte had always liked Misty. She often brought Misty coffee in the morning and spent extra time chatting with her. She was the first line of defense at the office, and Charlotte knew many of the parents could be difficult and downright rude at times. Misty handled the encounters gracefully, but Charlotte could see it took a toll at times. "I need some information."

"What is it?"

"I have a friend who wants to apply to teach at the school. I told her what a wonderful place it is. But she's getting out of a difficult marriage and needs a job with good benefits. Do you mind giving me an overview of the benefits package?"

"Well, we have a 401K plan, good health insurance, and life insurance."

"That's great. Do you know who the life insurance is through? Her husband works for one of the insurance companies, and let's just say she wants to make sure he can't find her."

"Oh, my. I see. Hold on, let me take a look. Um, here it is. Provident Casualty."

"Great. Thanks so much, Misty. You take care."

"You too, Charlotte."

She looked up the number for Provident and asked for one of the claims adjusters.

"James Whittaker. May I help you?"

"Yes, Mr. Whittaker. My name is Charlotte Fleming, and I'm calling because I suspect a claim you settled might be fraudulent."

"Which claim is that?"

"It concerns that terrible bus accident on the Bay Bridge last November. There were three or four employees of the Windsor School whose policies would have been paid out. One of them was Penelope Watson. But I believe Ms. Watson is still alive. I wanted to make sure that a death benefit wasn't paid out to her sister."

She could hear keys clicking. "Watson with one t?"

"Yes."

More clicking. "I see that there were two claims from that accident but nothing for Ms. Watson."

"Are you sure?"

"Yes, quite sure."

"Okay, thank you."

Another indication that Penelope hadn't been on that bus. Her sister would have claimed the death benefit if Penelope had died. She needed to find Nora Watson. Charlotte still hadn't heard back from the woman she'd sent a Facebook message to about the birthday party. She'd decided to take matters into her own hands. She'd gone earlier that day to the police department to tell them her theory. A kind detective listened patiently, his face impassive, not betraying what he was thinking.

"I'm so sorry for everything you've been through, Mrs. Fleming. It's unimaginable. You say the picture you saw took place in a bookstore in Florida?"

She nodded.

"If there's any credence to your theory, you would need to get the FBI involved. I can give you the number of the local field office."

She'd gone home and made the phone call, and the agent answering the phone took down the information.

"I'll forward this report to the appropriate squad. An agent will reach out to you shortly."

Now all she had to do was tell Eli.

Harper was doing homework at a friend's and wouldn't be home until around nine. As soon as Eli walked in, Charlotte handed him a glass of wine and told him they needed to talk. She'd put out an assortment of cheeses and nuts and opened his favorite cabernet, hoping to put him in a more receptive frame of mind. She'd even lit some candles and put on some soft background music.

"What's this all about?"

"I want to end the cold war," she said, arching an eyebrow.

He took a sip of the wine and sat down at the island.

"There's no war, honey. We're on the same side," he said.

"I know. Listen, I found out some things today that support my suspicions that Sebastion is alive."

"What things?"

"For one thing, Sebastion's teacher called both of us from her cell phone about an hour and a half before the accident occurred. I didn't even notice the missed call because I had all those calls from school, and then the news . . ."

"Hmm, I'll admit that's weird."

"Did you talk to her that day?"

"What? Of course not. I would have told you."

"Well, did she leave you a voicemail? The phone records show an eleven-second call."

His face paled. "Charlotte, what is this? Why are you rehashing all this now?"

She continued. "I thought maybe Sebastion got sicker that day, and Penelope was calling to let us know he couldn't go on the field trip. She could have told the bus driver to go without them and taken him to an urgent care or something." She didn't mention that she'd already called all the ones in the immediate area to no avail.

"But if she didn't reach us, she would have had to go ahead and get back on the bus. I mean, she wouldn't have the authority to take him anywhere on her own. Plus, she wouldn't have had a car," he said.

"I thought of that too, but she could have called an Uber. But that's not all. I found out that the life insurance on her was never paid out."

"How did you—"

"I called Misty at the school, and she gave me the name of their insurance carrier. So, I called them to check. Anyway, don't you think it's suspicious that the benefit wasn't paid?"

"I don't know. Did Penelope have a family? If no one called to make a claim—"

"She has a sister. I'm trying to locate her. I looked over the accident report. There were three teachers on that trip and three adult chaperones. The diagram showed fatalities in all the occupied seats. There were four empty children's seats, and the bus driver's seat was empty, as was one other adult seat. I don't think any of the other adults would have tried to get out before helping the children. What if Penelope was never on the bus?"

He blew out a breath. "That's a lot of conjecture. Honey, this could all be nothing. I would love to believe that our boy is still alive. You're pinning your hopes on a picture that is most likely just a boy who looks like ours. I'm worried about you."

"Don't you see all these red flags? The stop at McDonald's for all that time. The phone calls to us. Something's not right."

He took her hand in his. "Sweetheart, this is all very far-fetched. And the phone calls were probably because she wanted to give him something for his stomachache. She and Sebastion must have been on the bus, otherwise, why wouldn't Penelope have brought him home?"

"That's exactly what I intend to find out. First of all, if Penelope and Sebastion didn't get on the bus but somehow got hurt or lost, then Penelope's sister would have assumed she died in the crash and would have claimed the money. I told you, there was no insurance payout on Penelope."

"Who knows why the insurance wasn't paid. Maybe Penelope's sister didn't know about the policy. You have to stop this. All you're going to do is dredge up more pain, and like I said, jeopardize the insurance payout. Then where will we be left?"

She gave him a steely look. "I'm not giving up on our son, and I don't understand how you can."

CHAPTER
ELEVEN

Charlotte sat across the table from Agent Jamie Preston in the Violent Crimes Against Children squad at the Baltimore FBI field office. When the agent first walked in, Charlotte was surprised at how young she was. Even with her hair pulled back in a tight bun and minimal makeup on, she was attractive. Charlotte estimated her to be in her late twenties or early thirties. She wondered how long she'd been on the job.

"Thank you for agreeing to see me," Charlotte said. "I got the feeling from the first agent I spoke with that my concerns might not be taken seriously."

Agent Preston's eyebrows went up slightly. "I'm sorry the agent made you feel that way. We get a fair number of reports from people thinking they see their missing child that turn out to be false leads. But, please, tell me why you believe that your son is alive."

Charlotte told her about the phone calls, the unscheduled stop at McDonald's, and what she'd discovered about Penelope Watson's life insurance not being paid out.

Preston arched an eyebrow. "And you found out about the insurance, how?"

Charlotte shrugged. "I may have lied to the insurance agent, but I'm telling you, something doesn't add up. I know my son is alive, and for some reason, Penelope Watson took him." She leaned forward, making eye contact. "Do you have children, agent?"

Preston pursed her lips as if deciding whether or not to share personal information, then nodded. "Yeah, I have a son. A little younger than yours."

"Well, try to put yourself in my place. What would you do? At the very least, can't you look into Penelope? See if there's any evidence that she's alive? I think she's in Florida, so that's a start."

"Okay, let me see what I can find out. You said Ms. Watson called you from her cell phone. Do you have that number?"

Charlotte pulled out her phone. "Yes, I took screenshots to show my husband. Here." She handed her the phone, and the agent copied down the number. Preston returned the phone to her.

"Okay, Mrs. Fleming. I'll get back to you as soon as I have something."

"Thank you. And please, call me Charlotte."

The agent smiled for the first time and nodded. "Okay, Charlotte. And again, I'm deeply sorry for what you're going through. I'll get back to you soon."

"Oh, one more thing I forgot to mention. I did track down the woman who tagged the bookstore in the picture. I found her on Facebook. Unfortunately, her Facebook privacy settings didn't let me see much. I sent her a Facebook message telling her what happened and asking her to contact me, but I haven't heard from her."

"I wish you hadn't done that."

Charlotte bit her lip. "I know. I realized too late that all I may have done is alert Penelope to the fact that I had seen that picture."

"If you're right and this woman is alive and has your son, she's fabricated some story to explain how she came to have him. He's not a baby, so she would worry that he might tell someone she's not his mother. Please don't do anything else. Let us handle things from here on in."

As Charlotte drove home, she felt hopeful for the first time in almost a year. Regardless of how young Agent Preston was, Charlotte was grateful that her case had been assigned to her. If anyone could empathize, it was another mother—especially one with a son close to Sebastion's age.

When she walked into the house, Harper was doing her homework at the kitchen table, and Eli was chopping vegetables. She'd lied to him and told him she was meeting with Patricia about her new client. She didn't want to listen to him lecture her again. Why was he so opposed to turning over every leaf? She couldn't understand it.

"Hey, guys," she said, walking over to Harper and kissing her on the head. "Smells good," she told Eli, forcing herself to sound amicable.

"I'm making your favorite. Teriyaki chicken stir fry."

"Great. I'm gonna go change." She still barely had an appetite, but now it was more from anticipation and nerves than grief. She played scenarios over in her mind. If Penelope had Sebastion, that hopefully meant no harm would come to him. Charlotte knew that Penelope wasn't married, but maybe she had been at some point. Who knew, she could have lost a child and was in some sort of delusion about Sebastion. You heard stories all the time about women kidnapping pregnant women and stealing their babies. Had she planned it or had it been a crime of opportunity? Charlotte felt like she would go crazy until she could do something. She had prepared to fly down to Florida and confront the bookstore lady, insisting that she give her the name of the woman throwing the party. But if Agent Preston believed her, waiting and following her lead would be much better.

It took all the acting skills Charlotte could muster to get through dinner and small talk with Eli and Harper. She volunteered to clean up, and instead of joining Eli in the living room after dinner, she pled a headache and went upstairs.

She climbed into bed and prayed that tomorrow would bring good news.

CHAPTER
TWELVE

Charlotte had just dropped Harper off at school when she got the call. "Hello?"

"Agent Preston here. I have some information."

Her heart began to beat faster. "Yes."

"I was able to get a warrant for Ms. Watson's cell phone. The day the bus accident occurred, she called an Uber after she called you and your husband."

"I knew it! Where did she go?"

"We don't have that information yet. We're working on obtaining that information from the company and getting the driver's name. Her phone was active for two days after the accident."

"So, she's alive!"

"Well, we can't know for certain yet. She might have lost her phone, and someone else picked it up and used it, although it's unlikely since it would have been password-protected. But if we find the Uber went to her address, or if the Uber driver can confirm that she was with your son, we're in business."

"Even without either of those, you have enough to dig further, right?"

"Definitely. I'm working on getting a warrant to look into Ms. Watson's financials. We can see if there's activity in her bank accounts.

And I'll go to Florida to speak with the bookstore owner and the woman who hosted that party."

"Great. I'll book my ticket and meet you there."

"Hold on. I need you to stay home. I'll keep you updated every step of the way, but I can't have you there."

"But—"

"Charlotte. I get that this must be killing you. But the last thing we need is for you to jeopardize the investigation. I will do everything in my power to return your son to you. You have to trust me. Please."

"Okay, when are you leaving?"

"I'm flying out this afternoon."

She ended the call and drove home. She called Eli on the way and breathed a sigh of relief that it didn't go to voicemail.

"Everything okay?" he asked.

She was momentarily remorseful, realizing she never took the time to call and check in with him during the day anymore. "Yeah. I have to go meet with the clients in person. I'm flying to North Carolina today," she lied. "Can you pick up Harper? I'm sorry to drop this on you last minute, but they liked my proposal so much that they decided to increase the budget. They want to meet in person first." The truth was, she had called Patricia and told her she couldn't take on the work right now, but Eli didn't know that.

"Shoot. I've got a client meeting too. I can ask Madison if that's okay with you."

She couldn't worry about Madison right now. "Yes, that's fine. Tell her I said thank you."

"When will you be back?" he asked.

"Not sure. In a day or two. I'll call you from there."

"All right. Safe travels. Love you."

"Love you too."

She pulled into the driveway, ran into the house, and went straight to her laptop.

Then she booked a flight to Orlando.

PART TWO

PENELOPE

CHAPTER
THIRTEEN

"Tell me the story again about how a bad mommy took care of me until you saved me and became my new mommy." Sebastion looks at me with those big blue eyes, and my heart melts.

"I knew I should be your mommy from the first time I met you. Your birth mommy wasn't a nice mommy. She didn't have time to play with you and made you go to school when you didn't feel good. She got tired of you and left you. I was so happy when I was able to rescue you. You were so happy too. Now we play together all the time, and nothing is more important to me than you."

"And you'll never leave me, right?"

I push a golden curl from his forehead. "Never."

"How come I don't get on the school bus like the other kids on the street?"

I smile at him. "Because you're lucky. You get to stay home and be homeschooled. You know I used to be a teacher at a school. But I'd much rather stay home and teach you."

He yawns, and his eyes close. "I love you, Mommy," he mumbles as he drifts off to sleep, and I lean over to kiss his cheek. I wait a few minutes to make sure he's asleep before I slip from the room.

When I go downstairs, I see a message on my phone. It's from Rebecca.

Call me. I'm sorry but Sofi posted a picture from the party. I think the woman you're hiding from saw it.

My stomach drops, and I call her right away. "What's going on?"

"I'm so sorry, Cathy. Sofi didn't know and tagged the bookstore with a photo of the kids at Daniel's birthday party. Sebastion's birth mother called the store to try and get my information, but fortunately, Edith didn't give it to her. But then I got a Facebook message from a Charlotte Fleming. It's from a few days ago. I'm not on Facebook every day, so I just saw it. Her message said that her son was kidnapped. Is Charlotte her name? Sebastion's mom who lost custody?"

I could kill Sofi. I've been so careful. I've limited our social circle to a few other homeschool families. I never let anyone take Sebastion's picture. And in an instant, that moron, Sofi, has undone it all. "Yes, that's her. I need to think. Don't answer her message yet. I'll call you back."

"Okay. And again, I'm so sorry. I should have briefed Sofi on the situation. I wasn't thinking with all the hustle and bustle that day."

"It's not your fault," I say, even though I'm equally as pissed at her. Why did she have to invite an outsider to the party? "Okay, I'll call you back shortly." I run to my bedroom and start packing. There's no option. We have to leave.

CHAPTER FOURTEEN

Before
10 Months Earlier

I pay close attention to the children entrusted to my care. I've always known I wanted to be a teacher. From the time I was a little girl and my sister, Nora, and I played school, I had to be the teacher, she the student. Pre-K is the best. They're so sweet and eager, wide-eyed, innocent, just wanting to love and be loved. The Windsor School is the top preschool in Annapolis and a feeder school to the sought-after Charter Academy. It took me a little while to get used to the mothers. I didn't grow up with a silver spoon in my mouth, far from it, and these women may as well be from Mars.

I read an article once that said emotional poverty is just as damaging as financial poverty. After five years of working here, I can attest to the truth of that statement. More often than not, I don't even meet the mothers until parents' night since the nannies typically drop their children off. Every week there is a slot for a parent to come in and read, do a craft, or be a general day volunteer. I pay special attention to those mothers who can't find the time. I don't let the dads off the hook either, but I'm a realist. Most of these women don't work outside the home, whereas the husbands mostly do.

I've always been on high alert when it comes to my students. I closely observe the interactions between the parents and look beyond the superficial. I've had to call DCF several times when it turned out to be unsubstantiated, but better to be safe than sorry. The headmaster got angry and warned me that if I continued to report parents so quickly, he would fire me. I warned him that if he tried to prevent me from carrying out my obligation to report, I'd report *him*, and he would be the one out of a job. After that, he backed off. I wish someone had called DCF when I was growing up.

I can't remember a time from my childhood when my mother wasn't drunk. She'd start hitting the bottle the second my father left for his job at the bank. He was what you'd call a functioning alcoholic and didn't start drinking until he got home from work. Nora, seven years older than me, was the one who made sure I was up and dressed for school so that I could catch the bus on time.

I was eighteen when my parents died in a crash with my drunk father behind the wheel. I won't pretend I was sad. The insurance money paid for my college, and after Nora and I inherited and sold the house—we couldn't wait to leave it and the terrible memories behind—we each ended up with a lot more money than we expected. Over two hundred thousand each. I consider it restitution, although the damage those two did to us could never truly be repaid.

Today is the day all three pre-K classes are going to the Audubon Center. We've all been looking forward to it for weeks. My one misgiving is having to cross the Chesapeake Bay Bridge. There's a reason it's rated the second scariest bridge in the world. It's always reminded me of those tinker toys—the steel you can see through makes it a terrifying journey. It's just over 4 miles long and over 350 feet tall.

Everyone is ready to go, but Sebastion isn't here yet. I'm about to call Charlotte when she rushes in, pulling him behind her. Why can't the woman ever be on time? I frown when I notice that he's bent over, his little hand across his tummy as though in pain. I walk over to her.

"What's wrong, Sebastion? I thought you were excited to go to the Audubon Center today."

"Tummy hurts," he says, looking up at me with those beautiful blue eyes.

"I need to talk to Ms. Watson for a moment. Go play, and I'll see you later." Charlotte pushes him in the direction of his friends and in a low voice asks to speak to me off to the side. She brushes his pain off as psychosomatic, claiming he's been extra needy and that his doctor says it's a coping mechanism. But I know Sebastion, and he's not a faker. If he says his tummy hurts, then it does. I do my best to modulate my voice to keep my annoyance from it, but she's barely looking at me as she checks a text that's come in on her phone. She's too self-absorbed and self-important for my facial reactions to register.

"It's going to be a long day. Are you sure he's up to it?"

She shakes her head. "Yes, I know he'd regret missing it. Once I'm gone, he'll be fine." She looks over to see Sebastion laughing with another boy and seems relieved.

I'm still fuming when she leaves. I call him over to me and put my hand on his head. He's not warm. I pull out the forehead thermometer just to be safe, and his temperature is normal. Maybe she's right and it is stress-related, but that makes little sense to me. He'd been looking forward to the field trip as much as the rest of the class, so I don't think he'd fake an illness to get out of it.

Angela, another teacher, comes into the room and claps her hands. "Time to line up," she says, and turns to me. "All set?"

I nod and lead the children outside and onto the bus. Usually, Sebastion would sit next to his best friend, Josh, but I decide to sit next to him to keep a closer eye on him.

"I'll sit by the window, and you can sit on the aisle with Josh on the other side. That way you can still talk. Okay?"

He nods and slides in. I'll turn away from the window as we go over the bridge, or Sebastion won't be the only one who feels sick. Everything seems fine at first, but then, a few miles before the bridge, he starts crying and doubles over.

"I have to go potty. My stomach hurts really bad."

"Okay, sweetie. We'll stop."

I motion to Angela to tell the driver. Fortunately, a McDonald's is coming up in a mile.

She walks back down the aisle. "The driver's not happy about the unscheduled stop, but he says he'll pull over if you're quick."

When we stop, I usher Sebastion out and notice several more students follow us off the bus. The power of suggestion.

I take Sebastion into the women's bathroom and wait outside. I don't want to rush him, but he's been in there a long time, and I'm getting concerned about the bus driver.

"Honey, are you okay?"

The toilet flushes, and he comes out. He's as white as a sheet, sweat on his brow. There's no way he can make it through the field trip. Why hadn't his foolish mother listened to me? We walk back outside, and the driver stands by the door, his face red, tapping his foot.

"We are way behind schedule here."

"He's sick. We need to go back."

"What? Lady, are you kidding me?"

Angela comes down from the bus. "What's going on?"

"Sebastion's sick. Let me call his parents and see if they can come here and pick us up."

The driver shakes his head and rolls his eyes. "Hurry up."

I shoot him a dirty look. I'm reporting him to the bus company when we get back. I pull out my parent contact list and call Charlotte's phone first, which goes right to voicemail. Seriously? You send your sick kid on a field trip then ignore the teacher's call? Talk about shitty priorities. Next, I try her husband's office. It goes to voicemail too. I call his cell, and after four rings it's answered. By a woman.

"May I speak with Mr. Fleming?"

"Sorry, he's not available at the moment. Can he call you back?"

I can hear a shower running in the background. What a great husband and father. Instead of working, he's out screwing around. Both Angela and the driver are looking at me expectantly. I hate for the other children to miss the trip, but poor Sebastion needs to get home. That's when I make a split-second decision. I turn away and end the call then pretend to speak with Sebastion's father. "Hello, Mr. Fleming, this is Penelope Watson from Sebastion's school. Everything's okay, but he's not feeling well. Would it be okay for me to wait here with him until you can come pick us up and let the bus go on ahead?" I turn back around, nod at Angela and the driver, and point to the bus.

"Go on without us. Sebastion's father is going to come and pick us up," I tell them.

They get on the bus and drive off. What I've done is against protocol, but under the circumstances, I'm sure everyone will understand. If Charlotte Fleming tries to give me a hard time about it, I'll report her to DCF for neglect. I order an Uber on my phone, and ten minutes later, a car pulls up.

We're halfway back to school when the news alert comes through on the driver's radio. There's two-way traffic on the bridge because they've closed one side. A truck collided with a school bus, and they both careened off the bridge. It feels like all the air leaves my lungs. The children. Oh my God, the children! Then it hits me, what we've just escaped. It's a miracle! It takes me only a moment to decide. I lean forward and speak to the driver.

"Change of plans." I give him my home address.

CHAPTER
FIFTEEN

When the driver approaches my apartment building, Sebastion looks at me with confusion.

"You said we were going back to school."

I sneak a look at the driver, worried he'll get suspicious. I turn to Sebastion. "We are honey. I just need to get something from my apartment." We get out of the car, and I take his hand in mine. "How's your tummy?"

He shrugs. "Okay."

"Are you hungry? I have cookies."

He nods.

Once we get inside, I have to think fast. I sit him down in the kitchen with some Oreo cookies and milk. "I'll be back in a minute, sweetie." I go to the bedroom and turn on the news. I watch in horror as the anchor relays the details of the crash. Everyone is believed dead. There is no one left alive who can tell anyone that Sebastion and I never got back on the bus. Everyone will think we're both dead. It's a miracle! If Charlotte hadn't sent him to school sick, I would have been on that bus. My life would be over. And if I hadn't taken the initiative to call that Uber instead of putting him on the bus, we'd both be dead. This is the universe giving us both a second chance and sending me a message—Sebastion and I were meant to be together.

Charlotte and her husband will feel devastated when they get the news, of course. But it's only because of *my* concern for Sebastion that he's been spared. It was Charlotte's selfishness and ambition that put him on that bus to begin with. What kind of mother sends her sick child to school just so that she can go to work? If she needed the money, that would be one thing. But no one at the Windsor School needs the money. If you can afford to pay nearly fifty thousand dollars for a pre-K program, you are certainly not living paycheck to paycheck. Charlotte Fleming swept in late more often than not, wearing designer clothes, her hair and makeup perfect, driving her Range Rover, and living in the lap of luxury in one of most sought-after neighborhoods in Annapolis.

Poor Sebastion was simply an accessory to her. No more important than her designer purse. And I could swear there were times I smelled alcohol on her breath. What other jeopardy might she put him in if I send him back to her? No, he's safer with me. I'll devote myself to him. And besides, I'm betting that her marriage isn't long for this world with that cheating shit she's married to. I think back to all the nights I cried myself to sleep listening to my parents fight. How scared I was that my father's explosive temper would vent itself on me. Sebastion deserves better.

I pull a suitcase from the closet and throw in some essentials, including the five hundred dollars in emergency cash I keep on hand. I look around the room, debating what to leave and what to take. There can be no indication that I've been here, of course. It has to look like I perished in the crash. I open my jewelry box and grab the gold necklace Nora gave me when I graduated from high school. There's a photo of us on the wall, but I have to leave it, otherwise its absence will be noticed. I have to hurry. If any of my neighbors see me, it's all over. *Think, think*, I tell myself. We need to get out of the state, far from Maryland, where no one will remember that our names are listed as casualties from the accident. It's not as though I can manufacture a new identity right away, so we need to go somewhere no one knows us until I figure out what to do. That's when I decide on Florida. I need time to come up with a believable explanation as to why I suddenly have a four-year-old boy living with me. And I need time to make Sebastion forget where he came from. Orlando is perfect. A few hours from Nora's house in Stuart. Plus, Disney. Sebastion will love that. His favorite character is Buzz Lightyear. We'll have so much fun exploring the park together.

When I come out of the bedroom, he's standing by the door. "I want my mommy. Can you take me home?"

"Oh, sweetie. Your mommy just called and asked me to look out for you a little longer. She has to work."

His face falls. "She always has to work."

I walk over to him and crouch down so we're eye to eye. "I'm sorry, sweetie. I know it's hard. But in the meantime, we can go on a little adventure until you can go home. Have you heard of Disneyworld?"

"Yeah. My mommy and daddy said they would take me there for my next birthday."

"How would you like to go now?"

His face lights up. "Really?"

"Really. Your parents will meet us there. But it's a long ride, so we'd better get going."

"Okay."

I load him in the car, and we take off. When I first bought my used car, I was annoyed that it had built-in booster seats. Now I see it as another sign that this was meant to be. We'll be in Orlando by early afternoon tomorrow if I drive straight through. I'll rent a room for a few days, buy him some clothes and toiletries, and then figure out our next move. It's not long before he falls asleep, and as I drive us farther from Maryland, a picture begins to form in my mind. I'll find us a cute little house to rent, one with a pool. We'll join a local homeschool group so that Sebastion will have friends, but no documentation will be needed. I'll miss teaching at the Windsor School, but fate has a higher calling for me.

Thanks to my background in early childhood education, I know that in a few years, his memories formed up to now will be forgotten. As long as I'm patient and reinforce the new narrative, he will come to believe it. In the short term it's going to be challenging, but I just have to keep reminding myself that he'll be better off in the long run. If only someone had rescued me, I would have been spared a lifetime of pain. While I may not have hard proof that Sebastion's parents are actually abusive, I have enough evidence that they are neglectful. And that's just as bad. I'll give him all the love and support I never got growing up. And when the time is right, he and I will move closer to my sister, where he'll have three cousins. Everything is going to turn out just fine.

CHAPTER
SIXTEEN

Sebastion won't stop crying.

I want my mommy is the only sentence he's uttered for the past two hours. Fortunately, he was asleep when I checked us into the motel. The last thing I need is for someone to call the authorities thinking I've kidnapped him.

"It's time for me to tell you the truth," I say. We can't go anywhere in public until he accepts me as his new mommy.

He rubs his eyes and looks at me. He seems so small sitting in that big chair, and all I want to do is hug him and tell him everything will be all right.

"Your mommy doesn't want you anymore," I say, watching to see how he'll react.

"You're lying. I want my mommy."

"I'm sorry, sweetheart. Your mommy only has time to take care of your sister. She said she never wanted to have you. That you were a mistake and she tried to love you but she couldn't. But I do love you. I want to be your mommy."

Confusion fills his face and he starts to cry again. "My mommy loves me!"

I walk over to him and kneel down, taking his little hands in mine. "I'm sorry, but she doesn't. But I do."

"No, I don't want you."

He turns away from me and begins to sob. I sigh, stand up, and let him be. He needs time to grieve, but he'll come around. I go into the bathroom and put some makeup on, trying to figure out how to comfort him. An idea comes to me. I walk over to him again, handing him a box of tissues.

"Here, sweetie. Dry your eyes. Listen to me. If you'd rather be with the mommy who doesn't want you, I'll take you back to her. All I ask is that you stay with me until Christmas. What do you think?"

He shakes his head. "No. I want her now."

"Okay, let me call her."

I pick up my cell phone and dial my own number. After a moment, I speak. "Hello, Charlotte. It's Penelope. Sebastion doesn't believe that you don't want to be his mommy anymore. Can you talk to him?" He runs over, his hand extended. I make a face. "What? Please. No, Charlotte, wait—" I shake my head. "I'm sorry, honey. She hung up. She said she doesn't want to talk to you. That she's tired of taking care of you, and she has to get back to work." I feel horrible telling him this lie, but it's the only way. He'll be much happier once he accepts that I'm his true mother, ready to unselfishly devote myself to him.

He crumples in front of me, and I open my arms. He falls into them, crying softly. I rub his back. "It's okay, it's all going to be okay."

I open my laptop and navigate to the Disney website. "Look, sweetie, we can go here soon. Look at all the fun rides. And I bet we can even have breakfast with Buzz Lightyear!"

"Okay," he says, but there's no enthusiasm in his voice. He looks shell-shocked. My poor child.

"Are you hungry? Why don't I order something?"

He shakes his head and climbs up on the bed, curling into a ball. I turn on the television and find a show I think he'll like. He just needs time, I tell myself. Soon, he'll be back to the happy little boy I love. I pick up my book on childhood trauma and read.

CHAPTER
SEVENTEEN

After three trying months, Sebastion has finally turned a corner and accepted me as his mother. We rent a cute house in Campbell, Florida, only twenty-seven miles from Disney. It's fully furnished and in a quiet neighborhood. To help Sebastion adapt to his new life, we went to the pet store and picked out a guinea pig. Sebastion named him Buzz after Buzz Lightyear, of course. He's black and white and just the cutest little thing. Growing up, I was never allowed to have a pet, so this is a treat for me too. Maybe when we have our own house, we'll get a dog. I feel like I'm living in a Norman Rockwell painting. Every few days, he still asks about Charlotte, but it's getting easier and easier to distract him from his memories. The most important thing is that he calls me Mommy when we're out in public. I made it clear to him that if he gave anyone any reason to suspect that I wasn't his mommy, they would take him away and put him in an orphanage, where he would be until he grew up. I hate to use a scare tactic, but it's for his own good.

Tomorrow is Christmas and Sebastion is as excited as, well, a kid on Christmas Day.

"Shall we decorate the tree?" I ask while he's working on his spelling words in the kitchen. He looks up, holding his pencil midair, and nods. Sliding off the chair, he pushes his work away and follows me into the living room, where boxes of newly purchased ornaments sit open. Next to them is a box filled with the handmade ornaments we've been working on all month. Sebastion goes to that box first and grabs the reindeer made from Popsicle sticks and googly eyes.

"Where should I put Rudolph?" he asks.

"Wherever you like," I say, smiling at him.

He puts it on a low branch. Christmas music is streaming on a speaker from my phone, and a sense of happiness fills me. This is the first Christmas since Nora got married and moved away that I have a sense of belonging, of having my own family. "Jingle Bells" starts playing, and Sebastion drops the ornament in his hand and stares blankly.

"What's wrong?" I ask him.

"My mommy and daddy sang this to me when we went sledding." His lip starts to tremble. "I wanna go home."

I put my arms around him. "You are home, remember?"

He struggles from my embrace and runs from the room. I hear his bedroom door slam, and I sigh. It's his first Christmas in his new family, so he's still adjusting. I need to make this one extra special and create new memories with him that he'll cherish. He's so young; those old memories will be gone in a few years and all that will remain are the ones we make together.

I think back to the earliest Christmas I can remember. I think I was seven. I still believed in Santa Claus and asked my parents to leave him cookies and milk. My mother said she would and hurried me off to bed, warning me that if I didn't go to sleep, Santa wouldn't come. I was too young to know whether or not my parents were drunk back then. I only have scattered visions of that night. I remember sneaking downstairs after everyone was asleep to see if she'd left the cookies and milk by the fireplace. She had forgotten. Worried that Santa might not leave us anything, I went into the kitchen to do it myself. I had to climb on the counter to reach the cookies, and I slipped. The cookie jar came crashing down, and there was broken glass everywhere. I froze at first, and then went to the garage to find a broom. When I opened the garage door, it set off the burglar alarm. The next thing I knew, my father ran into the kitchen with a gun in his hands, and when he saw me, he began to yell.

"What the hell are you doing?" The phone rang, and he answered and told the alarm company it was a false alarm. My mother came down to see what the ruckus was.

"You forgot to leave cookies and milk for Santa. I was just trying to reach the cookies," I explained.

My father turned to me, his face full of fury. "There is no damn Santa Claus. It's time you stopped believing these childhood fantasies."

"Marvin!" My mother looked at him in horror.

"There is too a Santa," I said.

He grabbed my hand and pulled me from the kitchen into the living room. "Look," he said, pointing to the tree. "See all those presents? Your mother and I did that. Not Santa. Now go to bed!"

That Christmas I lost my faith in more than Santa.

CHAPTER
EIGHTEEN

Sebastion hardly ever asks about his parents anymore. We've settled into a nice routine. Up at eight, breakfast, some playtime outside, then lessons from nine to eleven. Another play break, lunch, and free reading for an hour in the afternoon. I ordered a homeschool kindergarten curriculum online, and I love giving all my attention to just one student. As much as I loved teaching pre-K, I can see now that having my attention divided among twelve students didn't allow me to maximize learning for each of them. I can't imagine how children fare once they're in classrooms twice that size. I do miss the camaraderie with my fellow teachers, and I'm realizing that Sebastion needs the company of other children.

Our homeschool group thinks my name is Cathy Miller. Watching some YouTube videos on Photoshop and making a new birth certificate and a fake social security card was easy. That, plus the phone and utility bills in my new name, was all I needed to get a Florida driver's license. If Sebastion ever corrects me about my name, I'll remind my new friends that I had to change it to avoid his abusive birth mother finding us. I've told them that she lost her parental rights and that we need to stay off the radar in case she tries to kidnap Sebastion. To avoid a digital trail, I cut up all my credit cards and withdrew my entire inheritance from a North Carolina bank branch on the way down here. Installing a safe in the rental house was next on my list so that the two hundred thousand dollars would be secure. Swapping out my Maryland tags for Florida tags registered to Cathy Miller was the final step in starting my new life.

We joined the group in January, and we take field trips together, have park playdates twice a week, and get together for a few classes where we take turns teaching. It's really the best of both worlds. The one fly in the ointment is my fear that Sebastion's former parents will find us, but I'm confident I've done an excellent job impressing upon the mothers how important it is that his birth mother doesn't know where we are. Many women in the group are already leery of authority figures, some having been persecuted by the school board for homeschooling. I trust that I can count on their discretion. Today, we're meeting the group for lunch and a beach day at Cocoa Beach. Sebastion's been in his bathing suit since breakfast.

"Can we go now, Mommy?" he asks again as I clean up the breakfast dishes. It still thrills me to hear him call me that.

"We're not meeting everyone until eleven, but what if we take the morning off from our studies and head there now? We can bring our books and read under the umbrella."

He jumps up and down. "Yay!"

When we arrive, we set our things up on the beach, and after everything is ready, he grabs my hand and pulls me toward the water. "Come on, let's go swimming."

I grab the wet bag with my keys and wallet and strap it around my arm. You can never be too safe, and I'm not about to leave them on the beach where anybody could steal them.

We run into the water and have a splashing fight until I tire of all the water in my eyes. I start to get bored but can tell he's not ready to get out yet. To be honest, I really don't like swimming in the ocean. There are too many strange creatures. I much prefer a swimming pool. I watch him try to do a handstand, and we hold hands and jump when the small waves come. Finally, I can't take it anymore. "Time to get out."

"No," he says as he sticks his chin out defiantly.

I feel my temper surge. He's been a bit of a handful lately, and this rebellious streak is getting worse.

"Sebastion, it's enough already, Mommy's tired."

He turns and swims away from me, his legs kicking as fast as they can. In two strides, I'm behind him and I grab him around the waist to stop him.

"Let go of me," he shouts.

"Sebastion! If you don't stop this instant, we'll go home and forget the playdate."

"I hate you," he yells, and the heat rises to my face when I notice swimmers near us all looking at me.

Under my breath, I say, "Please be a good boy, and I'll buy you an ice cream." I know it's the absolute wrong thing to do, but I can't risk him causing a scene. The promise does the trick. He turns back to me, and we walk back to the beach.

"We have to go to the car and get my money," I tell him, wanting to talk to him where no one can hear us.

I open the door to the Volvo, and he climbs in the front seat, which I allow only because we're not driving. I get in on my side and shut the door.

"I'm extremely disappointed in your attitude, young man. It's not acceptable for you to speak to me that way. Especially in public."

He gives me a long look. "You promised ice cream."

"I know. But first you have to promise that you'll listen the first time, otherwise, the police might come and take you away. Little boys who sass their mommies can get in big trouble."

His eyes narrow, and his face turns red. "You're mean! My real mommy is nice."

It feels like all the breath whooshes out of me. "I'm your real mommy. How many times do I have to tell you that? I would never give you away like she did. But if you're not happy, I can take you to the orphanage. In fact, maybe we should go there now."

"No, no." He starts crying, his breath coming in uneven hitches.

I don't reach out to comfort him—not yet. He needs to learn that his words have consequences. "Well then, I don't want to ever hear another word about your old mommy. She doesn't love you. She doesn't want you. She's forgotten all about you. She even sent me a letter saying how happy her life is without you." In a few years, if he's still asking, I'll say they died, but I'm confident he'll forget.

His shoulders are shaking now, and I'm starting to worry he's getting hysterical.

"But I love you, Sebastion. I'll never leave you. I promise. It's not your fault. Your mommy is a bad person. She couldn't see what a wonderful little boy you are. I'm sorry I had to say all those things, but it hurts my feelings when you talk about her. Especially since I'm the one who loves you and takes care of you. Can you understand that?"

He nods, his tears still falling, but his chest no longer heaving.

"So do you promise to never, ever, talk about her again?"

"I promise."

"Okay, let's go get you that ice cream."

CHAPTER
NINETEEN

Now

My things are all packed and in the car. I'll take care of Sebastion's room tomorrow. I pick up my phone and call my sister.

"Hey there, how's it going?" she answers.

"Not so great. You remember I told you about Sebastion's birth mom getting out of rehab?"

"Yeah?"

"Well, she's tracked us down. I've already called my landlord and Venomed her one month's rent to terminate and said she could keep the security deposit. You know I always fulfill my obligations. I let her know that I deducted the cost of the carbon monoxide detectors I'd had to buy when we moved. She's lucky that I didn't report her for the violation."

Nora laughs. "Still making sure everyone follows the rules."

"You know my motto, rules are there to keep society in order. Can you book us a place to stay until we get settled? One of those places with a kitchenette, washer, and dryer? An Airbnb in your name so we don't have to show ID when we check in?"

"I guess so. I don't understand why you have to keep running like this. Sebastion's mom lost her parental rights. Couldn't you have her arrested if she tries to come near Sebastion?"

"It's not that. I don't want him getting all upset. It's taken me months to help him forget about her and embrace his new life with me. His therapist said it's imperative that she have no contact with him. It could really set him back. We've had to do so much work. It's why I haven't even brought him to meet you and the kids yet." There is no therapist, of course, but I've read enough books about this kind of thing to know that what I'm saying is true.

"Don't get mad, but are you sure it's good for him never to see her again? I don't mean for you to ever give her custody back, but he may want to know her one day."

Annoyance bubbles up, but I keep my voice even. "I'm not the one who terminated her rights. The court had good reason. You have to remember, he's a traumatized child. The first few years of his life were spent neglected and malnourished. Who knows who his mother had in and out of that horrible rattrap she lived in. I've had him for almost a year, and he's finally a happy little boy. Remember how Mom and Dad were and multiply that by a hundred. I'm never going to subject him to her influence again."

"I'm sorry. I didn't mean to be insensitive. When do you think you'll get here?"

"We'll leave in the morning. I haven't told Sebastion that we're moving yet. But I know when I tell him he'll meet more family, he'll be really excited."

"I can't wait to meet him, Pen. I still can't believe you're a mother!"

"You're going to love him. Listen, please remind Frank and the boys not to say anything about his being adopted."

"Okay, but don't you think you'll have to tell him one day? Is that really fair to him?"

I grind my teeth and sigh. "Of course he knows he's adopted. He wasn't a baby when I got him. But we don't talk about it anymore. We're leaving the past in the past. That's all I'm saying."

"Okay, okay."

I love my sister, but sometimes she can be so obtuse. We hang up, and I go to Sebastion's room. I gently nudge his shoulder. "Wake up, sleepyhead. I have a surprise."

He rubs his eyes and looks at me. "What?"

"We're going to meet your Aunt Nora, Uncle Frank, and . . . three cousins!"

"I have cousins?"

"Yes, all boys: Mario, Phillip, and Anthony. Anthony is only a couple of years older than you are."

"I don't remember them."

"You're going to have so much fun. They have a built-in pool and a trampoline. Come on, go brush your teeth and wash up."

He gets out of bed and goes into the bathroom. I rush to his closet and throw things into some suitcases.

When he comes out of the bathroom, I've already laid out a pair of shorts and a shirt for him.

He looks around the room and notices that his stuffed animals and the posters on the wall are gone.

"Where's my stuff?"

"I packed it. We're moving closer to my sister so we can be near family. About two hours away, in Stuart. You're going to love it."

"I don't wanna move. What about my friends and my classes?"

Damn that Sofi. I hate to uproot him again, but there's no way we can stay here. For all I know, Charlotte is already on her way here, and if she gets the authorities involved, it won't be hard to track us down.

"I know, honey. It's not easy to move. But you'll make lots of new friends, and we'll find a new homeschool group."

He stomps his foot on the ground and crosses his arms. "No. I like it here."

I think fast. The only thing I come up with is a way to appeal to the fear of the police I've instilled in him. "I do too, but the police are shutting down the homeschool classes because the school system is mad that we're homeschooling. The police lied and said the mommies were stealing things. If we don't leave, they'll think we're a part of it and arrest us too. They'll put me in jail, and you'll go to jail for little boys. We have to leave before they find us."

"Oh no!" he says as he grabs my hand. "I'm scared."

"It's okay. I'll always protect you, but we have to hurry and go now."

He helps me as we grab the last of our things and put them in the car. I lock the door and leave the key under the mat. I hope we'll have better luck in Stuart. If Charlotte discovers that he's still alive, she'll never stop until she finds him. She'll paint me as a criminal. But I'm just a woman doing her best to protect the child that fate determined should belong to her. I can't let Charlotte find us and take him back. He doesn't belong to her anymore.

We get in the car and drive off. We're almost to the end of the street when I notice a car pulling up to our house and parking. I press the gas and forge ahead.

PART THREE

CHAPTER
TWENTY

It took everything Charlotte had to wait in her rental car while Agent Preston went inside the Sunshine Bookstore. After twenty minutes, the agent emerged, and Charlotte got out of the car and walked over to her.

"Charlotte! What did I say about coming here?"

"I couldn't just sit at home. I was going crazy!"

"You have to stay out of my way. It's for your own good. Why can't you understand that—"

"Could you sit at home if it was your son?"

Preston's expression softened. "No. But it doesn't make it right. Fine, you're here. But you have to do what I say. Can you at least promise me that?"

She nodded. "Yes. I'll go back to my hotel after you tell me what she said."

"The woman who threw the party is Rebecca Halstead. She has a son named Daniel. I'm on my way to her house now. And no, you can't come. Go back to your hotel and wait for me."

"Please, let me just follow behind you. I'll stay in the car. I can't just sit in a room."

"I'm probably going to regret this. But if you get out of that car—"

Charlotte put her hands up. "I won't."

She followed behind the agent, and ten minutes later, they arrived at Rebecca's house, a pink bungalow in a well-maintained neighborhood. Charlotte watched as Preston knocked on the door, which was opened by a young woman who looked to be in her early thirties. She had a baby on her hip and a little boy beside her. Charlotte put her car window down so she could hear their conversation.

"Hello, ma'am. I'm Special Agent Preston, and I'd like to ask you some questions." She flashed her badge.

Rebecca opened the door, and they both went inside.

Charlotte drummed her fingers on the dashboard while she waited. The woman in there had seen her son. Was friends with Penelope. She'd know how Sebastion was doing—whether he seemed scared or hurt. Charlotte had a million questions, and what if Agent Preston didn't ask them? Almost on autopilot, she jumped out of the car, ran up the walkway to the house, and knocked on the door. A few moments later, Rebecca was back, looking puzzled.

"Can I help you?"

"I'm Agent Preston's partner. May I please come in?"

"Oh, sure."

Preston scowled. Her face turned red, but she quickly recovered.

"Sorry, had to take a call," Charlotte improvised.

"Take a seat, *Agent*," Preston said. "Mrs. Halstead was just identifying the children in this picture."

"This is Simon Logan, Matty Brennan, and this one is Sebastion Miller." She pointed to Charlotte's son.

"His name is Sebastion Fleming," Charlotte said. "He's my son."

There was a flicker of recognition on Rebecca's face. "Fleming, Fleming. Wait. You're the woman who messaged me?"

Agent Preston sighed loudly, shaking her head.

"Yes, you never answered me."

"What is this all about?" she said, suddenly defensive.

"I apologize for Mrs. Fleming's deception. But as a mother, I hope you'll understand. We have reason to believe that the woman claiming to be Sebastion's mother is a suspect in a kidnapping."

Rebecca's mouth dropped open. "So, what you wrote to me is true?" she asked Charlotte.

"How long have you known Ms. Miller?" Agent Preston asked.

"Little less than a year. Cathy joined our homeschool group in January. She said she'd adopted Sebastion from an abusive situation and that his mother had lost all her parental rights. She told us that his mother was dangerous and was looking for him. That's why I didn't answer your message."

"Did you inform Ms. Miller about the Facebook message you received?"

"Yes, because I believed her story and wanted to warn her. I'm sorry. I didn't know."

"When did you tell her?"

"Two days ago."

Charlotte pulled out her phone and tapped it. She showed the picture to the woman. "Is this the woman you call Cathy Miller?"

"Yes, that's her."

Charlotte turned to Preston. "That's Penelope Watson. Sebastion's preschool teacher."

Rebecca's hand flew to her mouth. "This is unbelievable! She kidnapped your son? Oh my God! She seemed like such a good mother. And he called her Mommy. I had no idea. I'm so sorry."

"How did he look? Did he seem happy? Is he healthy?" Charlotte's emotions were ricocheting between elation that her son was really alive and despair at what he must be going through. She was terrified she would never get him back.

"He seemed healthy." Rebecca tilted her head. "Happy? I don't know. He was always quiet, subdued. I thought he was just shy. He always stayed close to her and looked to her for approval before doing anything."

"What do you mean?" Charlotte asked.

"Like if someone brought cookies or other treats to the park playdates. Most of the kids would just run over to the table and grab them, but he always looked to her for a nod or okay. She definitely kept him on a tight leash, but I thought it was because she was worried about his mother finding him." She shook her head. "Now I know that's true but for the wrong reasons. You must be going crazy."

"You have no idea."

"Here's her address and phone number." She scribbled on a paper. "Her house isn't far from here. About four miles."

"Thank you," Agent Preston said, taking the paper. "And please keep this conversation to yourself for now. Don't tell any of the mothers. We can't risk her finding out that we're close. She'll spook and run."

Rebecca nodded. "Of course. Please let me know if there's anything at all that I can do."

After they'd left and Rebecca had shut the door, Preston whirled around and glared at Charlotte. "I hope you realize you may have cost us any chance of finding your son."

Her stomach dropped. "I'm sorry. I just needed to know—"

"I've been more than patient with you, but I've had it. How long do you think it will be before she calls one of her homeschool friends to share this choice gossip?" She shook her head. "We need to move fast. She's had a two-day lead on us. Hopefully, she's still in town. You stay out of my way, do you understand? Go back to the hotel. Now."

Tears filled Charlotte's eyes, and she nodded, got in the car, and drove off.

As Charlotte sat waiting in her hotel room, her excitement mounted at the thought of seeing her beloved son. What had Penelope told him? It was evident from what Rebecca had said that Sebastion had been brainwashed into calling her Mommy and was interacting with a whole group of children and mothers without ever mentioning who he really was. What the hell had Penelope done to her son? Charlotte had thought Penelope was such a great teacher. She'd respected the way Penelope prioritized her students over their parents, who were often entitled and spoiled, believing that the expensive tuition gave them the right to express every opinion. Now Charlotte searched her memory for signs of mental instability in the woman.

Charlotte had often felt Penelope's scrutiny when she'd drop Sebastion off in a hurry, but it hadn't struck her as pathological. The year before, when she'd had the luxury of staying at home, she would often linger for fifteen or twenty minutes, allowing Sebastion to set the pace for the separation. That raised the ire of his teacher, whose philosophy was that a clean break was best for everyone. The mother Penelope witnessed was, by necessity, a different one.

One day in particular, about a week before the accident, stood out.

At the beginning of the school year, Penelope had sent out an email with sign-ups for class reading. She'd prefaced it with the admonition that it was only for parents—no nannies. Charlotte had chosen a day and marked off the time on her work schedule. Unfortunately, her boss, an older man who probably never had to worry about anything child-related, rescheduled an important meeting. Charlotte had only been with the company a couple months and couldn't afford to make waves. It was too late to change the schedule, so her nanny would have to pinch-hit for her.

"I don't want Mandy to come and read today. Why can't you?" Sebastion had been in a melancholy mood.

She closed her eyes, took a deep breath, and put her hand on his shoulder. "Honey, I told you. My boss rescheduled a meeting for this afternoon, and I can't get out of it."

She'd dropped Sebastion off in the line but then parked in visitor parking. Dread filled her as she made her way to the classroom to let Penelope know the situation. Penelope was still greeting the children when she approached the classroom, so she stood outside, where Sebastion couldn't see her, and waited. A few minutes later, she poked her head in the classroom. Penelope waved her in.

"Is there something I can help you with?"

She tried to make it fast before her son caught sight of her. "I'm so sorry, but my boss moved a meeting around, and I can't do the reading time today."

Penelope stared at her for a moment, saying nothing, and then finally raised her eyebrows. "This is very last minute."

"I know. My nanny, Mandy, is happy to—"

"You know my policy. If you're too busy, I'll read to the children myself. But I have to say—"

"Mommy!" Sebastion ran over and threw his arms around her legs.

"Hi, sweetie. I was just talking to Ms. Watson for a minute. Give me a hug, and then go play."

"Did you change your mind? Are you going to read?"

That's when she saw the look on Penelope's face. A mix of disapproval and disgust.

"Your mommy has to work, but don't worry, we'll have her read another time. I'm sure she feels just terrible for disappointing you. I'll read today, so you still get to sit in the special reader's helper seat."

She felt that Penelope judged her, but she certainly would have never in a million years imagined she would go to these lengths.

Her phone rang. It was Agent Preston.

"Doesn't look as though anyone was inside the house. We're working on getting a warrant."

Anguish overcame her. "Do you think she's on the run? Rebecca told her about my message, so she knows I'm on to her."

"Now that we have her alias, we can track her down. The office is accessing her license and tag information. We'll put out a BOLO on her car. And we'll try to find her sister. I've got someone calling the school to get her emergency contact information. Hopefully, we'll get lucky there. We're also accessing the records on her new cell phone."

She was despondent. "What if we never find her?"

"We're going to. I promise."

But Charlotte knew all too well that some promises were impossible to keep.

CHAPTER
TWENTY-ONE

I left my cell phone in the car and bought a burner. Now Sebastion and I are waiting outside Walmart for the Uber I called using the new phone. I was only able to take two suitcases from the car. Unless I'm lucky and they don't figure out my identity, we'll have to part with the rest of our things. A man comes outside and throws his food wrapper on the ground. Ugh.

"Excuse me. That's littering!" I say, pointing to the trash.

He gives me an apathetic look and keeps walking. If I weren't in such a hurry, I'd call the cops and report him! Why can't people follow the rules? Still fuming, I call Nora while we wait.

"Hey, you almost here?" she answers.

"She found the house. We got away right before she spotted us. A minute later, and she would have seen us."

"Oh my gosh! Where are you now?"

"Waiting for an Uber to get to the Airbnb. Listen to me, if by some crazy chance she finds you, you can't tell her where I am. She might even have the police with her. She's a consummate liar."

"What? Why would the police believe her?"

"I'm just saying. I don't know. Call me paranoid but better to be safe. Just don't tell anyone where I am. And we're going to have to postpone getting together. I'm not sure where we're going, but it has to be out of state."

"Oh, Penelope. You've got to stop running. This woman is ruining your life. Just calm down. I'll come over later, and we'll figure something out together. Don't do anything rash."

"Okay."

"Promise me."

"I promise. Uber's here. Gotta go."

"Who saw us?" Sebastion asks as we're getting into the car.

"Nobody. Don't worry." I can't get into it in front of the Uber driver. Why couldn't Charlotte just leave well enough alone? Why couldn't she just enjoy the fact that she has the freedom to work as much as she wants now? No more struggling to get to school on time or making her child go to school sick so she doesn't miss one of her important meetings. It's not fair. Now I have to uproot my child from all he knows and loves because Charlotte is so selfish. A feeling of rage overcomes me, and I dig my nails into the palms of my hands. I want to scream with all my might.

"Do you have a booster seat?" I ask the driver.

"What? No."

I make a face. Can no one do anything right? "When I ordered the car, I put in the comments that I was riding with a young child. This is really unacceptable."

The driver shrugs. "Are you getting in or not?"

I shake my head. "Yes, but please be careful."

The seat belt is way too big for him, but I buckle the lap belt. I'd report the driver if I weren't trying to keep such a low profile. I count to one hundred in my head, hoping it will be enough to calm me down.

We arrive at the house without incident. The code to the lockbox works, and we get the key and go inside. It's a small bungalow, bright and airy, but close to the houses on each side. I feel exposed. The first thing I do is shut the living room curtains.

"Where are we? Is this our new house?" Sebastion asks.

"No, sweetie. We're just here for a couple days until we figure out where to go next. We need to get far away from here so police don't think we're part of those bad ladies stealing and arrest us."

He starts to cry. "I don't want to go to jail."

I pick him up and kiss the top of his head. "I'll keep you safe. I promise. We may need to change your name."

"No!"

"Okay, okay." He's clearly not ready for that. If it comes to it, I'll have to figure out a way to make it a fun game for him. "Never mind. It's all fine. How 'bout I order us a pizza and then we can go online and try to find a fun place to move."

"Okay."

I place an order through DoorDash. "Let's go sit on the sofa and look together," I tell him. He follows me over, and I put the computer on my lap. I pull up a map of the United States. "We're here," I tell him as I point to Florida. "I think we should go to the other corner of the map. Washington or Montana."

He begins to fidget. "I don't know."

"Okay, what's your favorite weather?"

"Sunshine and warm. Like here."

"What are your favorite things about Florida?"

"I like the beach. And the palm trees. And Disney."

"I've got it! Do you know what state has all of those things and is even prettier than Florida?"

He shakes his head.

"California!"

CHAPTER
TWENTY-TWO

Charlotte spent a sleepless night lying next to her phone, willing it to ring with good news, but it remained silent. She got dressed and went down to the restaurant for coffee. She thought she'd lose her mind if she stayed in the hotel room for another minute. She texted Eli that she was already in a meeting and would call him later that afternoon. She was in no mood to talk to him and make up more lies about her trip. Penelope was now going by the name Cathy Miller. She'd deliberately chosen a very generic name. The fact that she'd taken on a new identity meant she was well aware of what she was doing. She wasn't laboring under the delusion that Sebastion belonged to her. Instead, she had executed a plan to kidnap and keep him. Charlotte couldn't fathom how someone could be so cruel. To allow her to believe that her son was dead. If Penelope was that cold and calculating, who knew what she might do to Sebastion if she found out that they were close to finding her.

She drank two cups of coffee, her mind imagining all sorts of scenarios, when finally, her phone rang. She got up to find a spot to talk more privately.

"Did you find her?" Charlotte asked in lieu of a hello.

"Not yet. We tracked her cell phone, which was active until noon yesterday. Nothing since then. I'm assuming she bought a burner. We found her car in a parking lot by a Walmart. We're checking the security cameras in the area to see if someone picked her up or if she called for a car. I've got some agents reviewing the footage now."

"So now what? She dumped her phone and her car?"

"I'm going to speak with her sister. The school gave me her information. She was listed as Penelope's next of kin."

"I want to go with you."

"Absolutely not!"

"Hear me out. Penelope already knows we're on to her, so there's no risk of my revealing that. The sister might respond better if I'm there. Who knows what Penelope has told her. Remember what Rebecca said about the story of Sebastion's real mom being a drug addict and dangerous? If she sees for herself that I'm not that, she might tell us the truth."

"I don't know—"

"Honestly, what could it hurt at this point? Are you confident that you'll be able to convince her that Penelope was lying? I really think I need to be there."

Charlotte heard Agent Preston sigh. "All right. I'll swing by and get you. Be there in fifteen."

Charlotte went to her photo album on her phone and scrolled through, finding as many pictures of her and Sebastion as she could. She'd show them all to Penelope's sister as proof that she'd been a good mother to him. She stopped and ran her finger over a photo of the two of them—Sebastion sitting on her lap. She missed him so much it hurt. She ached to hold him again, to kiss his cheek, and to inhale the sweetness of his skin. Her baby. Dare she believe that she might bring him home?

CHAPTER
TWENTY-THREE

I call my sister. "Change of plans. We're leaving town today."

"What? I'm not even going to get to meet my nephew? Where are you going?"

"It's better if you don't know for now. I'll call you once we get settled. Sebastion's mom is in town, and I can't risk her finding us."

"I understand, but I'm so disappointed. The boys were really looking forward to meeting Sebastion too. How are you getting . . . Wait, someone's at the door. Be right back."

I hear voices in the background. Sounds like two women.

"Pen, I gotta go. It's the FBI! I'll call you back."

Panic seizes me. The FBI! How did they find Nora? That means they know I'm Cathy Miller. Shit, shit, shit! We need to get to the bus station fast. I'm about to order an Uber but then freeze. Can they track my phone? No, no, there's no way they could know my burner number. I go to a browser and look up the Greyhound schedule. The next bus leaving from the Florida Mall is at 2:10 pm. It's a sixty-eight-hour trip so it will take us two and a half days. This is going to be agony, but there's no other option. I'll turn it into an adventure. And really, it'll be educational. Think of all the states Sebastion will get to see. I'll pack lots of good snacks and some cozy blankets and we'll be fine. My anxiety subsides. This is a good plan. The trip will give me time to plan our next steps before we arrive in Los Angeles.

I'll find a motel that accepts cash and won't insist on identification. Now that Charlotte knows that Sebastion is alive, I'm going to have to come up with new identities for both of us, but it shouldn't be that hard now that I've done it once. And Mexico is close to California, so if worse comes to worst, we can disappear over the border and never be found. I'm quite sure two hundred K will be enough to keep us living in comfort there.

Sebastion is finishing up the French toast I ordered from Door-Dash with the prepaid credit card I bought. I pick up a fork and take a bite. "Yum. So, listen, buddy. We'll get going in a little bit and head to California. Isn't that exciting?"

"Uh-huh," he says, not taking his eyes off the show.

"I'll just pack up our stuff. When your show's over, I need you to get dressed. I'll put your clothes out on the bed."

As I gather our things together, I wonder if Charlotte is here too and how much she knows. I pick up my phone and call Rebecca.

"Hello?"

"Hi, Rebecca, it's Cathy."

"Don't you mean Penelope?" Her voice is cold.

"What?" I play innocent.

"Don't even. The FBI was here. I can't believe you kidnapped that child. His poor mother. Do you have any idea what you put her through? She's devastated."

So, Charlotte was here. "What did you tell them?"

"I'm not giving you any information. But you should turn yourself in. Sebastion doesn't belong to you. You're a horrible person and I hope—"

I end the call. Screw her. What does she know about horrible people? Charlotte probably charmed her with her beautiful face, expensive clothes, and perfect hair. *You already gave me all the information I need, Rebecca*, I mutter under my breath, making a face. This means that they have my old address and have already gone there. Luckily, I cleared out. But now they're at my sister's house. Will Nora believe Charlotte and give them this address? I can't chance it. I go to my Uber app and order a car.

I walk over to Sebastion and turn off the television.

"Hey!"

"Sorry, bud. But we have to go now. Throw on these clothes, no time to even brush your teeth. We need to leave."

Ten minutes later, we're in the car on our way to the bus station.

CHAPTER
TWENTY-FOUR

Charlotte and Agent Preston sat in Nora Rossi's kitchen. Nora had ushered them right in when Agent Preston identified herself.

"I know why you're here. It's Sebastion's mother, right? She's violating the restraining order?"

Charlotte was about to speak, but a stern look from Agent Preston stopped her. She took a deep breath and waited for Preston to speak.

"Actually, Mrs. Rossi, your sister's story about Sebastion is not accurate."

Her brow creased. "What do you mean?"

"Were you aware of the bus accident that claimed the lives of the students and teachers on a field trip last November? The accident your sister was believed to be in?"

"Of course! I didn't hear from her for two days afterward. I thought she was dead. She didn't end up going on the trip because she'd been in a car accident that morning and was unconscious for two days."

Agent Preston's brows went up. "You didn't think it was strange that she was listed as one of the casualties? Wouldn't the school have known she didn't come to school that day and wasn't on the trip?"

Confusion played over her face. "Well, now that you say that—um—at the time I was just relieved that she was okay; I didn't really question it. I think she explained it away by saying the news got the names off the roster or something. Anyway, what does it have to do with anything?"

"Sebastion was a student of your sister's. He was supposed to be on that field trip. In fact, your sister was not in an accident prior to the field trip and was on the bus. But we believe Sebastion got sick and they stopped at a fast-food restaurant. The bus continued without them. But no one knew that. They were both believed to be dead."

Charlotte watched Nora's face and saw the truth beginning to dawn on her. "Wait, are you saying she didn't adopt him from foster care? That he went to that fancy school where she taught?"

Agent Preston nodded. "Yes. We were able to access her phone records from that day. She took an Uber from McDonald's to her home. We interviewed the Uber driver and he identified her and Sebastion. She took him that day."

"Oh my God! Are you sure? Why? Why would she do that? This makes no sense."

Finally, Charlotte spoke. "Can I show you something?"

Nora nodded.

She pulled up the "favorites" album on her phone and handed it to Nora. "You can scroll through. I'm Sebastion's mother. Those are pictures of the two of us over the years. As you can see, I love him very much. I would never hurt him."

"Do you know where your sister is now?" Agent Preston asked.

Her hand flew to her mouth. "I booked her an Airbnb, but she called me just as you arrived. She knows you're here. She said they're leaving but wouldn't tell me where."

"Do you have the phone number she called from?"

Nora got up, grabbed her phone, and tapped it. "Here."

Agent Preston took a screenshot and then sent a text. "We'll track this and get a location. Give me the address of the Airbnb. She may have left something there that will help us."

Nora wrote it down and gave it to her. She turned to Charlotte. "I'm so sorry. I truly don't understand why she would do this. It must be some sort of a misunderstanding. My sister's a good person. Yes, she's had some issues in the past, but nothing like this. What's going to happen to her?"

"Let's just find them both first. If you think of anything else or if you hear from her again, please call me," Agent Preston said, handing Nora her card.

They left and got back into Preston's car.

"We'll check the airports and bus and train stations. My guess is she'll take a bus since that doesn't require any identification. But she could be getting sloppy."

"She could even hitchhike or have called someone to drive her. Then what? She could stay hidden forever," Charlotte said.

Agent Preston turned and looked at her, steely determination in her eyes. "She's not going to stay hidden. If I have to walk through hell and back, I'm going to find her."

CHAPTER
TWENTY-FIVE

We arrive at the bus terminal with time to spare. Sebastion is fidgety and cranky.

"I'm tired. And it's hot. I wanna go home."

"Why don't you read a book?"

He makes a face.

"Fine. You've already had too much screen time today, but I'll make an exception." I pull out my iPad and load one of his games. The Wi-Fi is turned off, so it can't be tracked. I hand it to him with earbuds, and he's blessedly content for now. No one tells you how hard parenting is, but most parents aren't under this type of stress. Once we're settled in Los Angeles, things will be great again.

My phone buzzes, and I look down. Nora. "Hey," I answer.

"Penelope! What have you gotten yourself into! The FBI is looking for you. They say you kidnapped that boy."

I look around the crowded station. "It's complicated. I can't really talk here. But it's not what you think. I rescued him."

"Honey, please come back. We can figure this out together. His mother is beside herself. She thought he was dead all this time. How could you do this?"

It occurs to me that they could be tapping this line now. What if Nora is cooperating with them? I end the call. I need to get rid of the phone. *Think, think.* We're sitting close to the counter, and I strain to hear where the woman at the window is going. She's going to New Jersey, and her bus leaves at the same time as ours. I watch as she struggles with her bags and wrangles two small children. Luck is with me as the group sitting beside us gets up and leaves. She takes their place. When her back is to me, I slip the phone into the front pocket of her purse. I'm getting really good at this. I should write my own book about disappearing one day. Five minutes later, they leave. Problem solved. That should divert them until we're on the bus headed to California.

I tap my foot, waiting for the minutes to pass, my eyes trained on the entrance as each new person walks in. Just another hour before we can board our bus. I'll make Nora understand. She'll be on my side when I explain what an absentee mother Charlotte was to Sebastion. How she sent him to school sick, how she was so cold when he wanted her attention. Also, my suspicions that she has a problem with alcohol. Nora won't be able to deny that he's much better off with me. She'll bring the boys out to see us after the trail has gone cold and the FBI has given up. I'll have to pick up another phone along the way. But for now, I'm relieved nothing in our possession can be tracked. We're almost home free.

CHAPTER
TWENTY-SIX

Agent Preston and Charlotte arrived at the bus station and parked.

"Stay behind me," Preston admonished as they approached the door. She'd gotten word that the cell phone was pinged here over an hour ago. They could only hope that Penelope's bus hadn't left yet. Charlotte watched as Preston looked at something on her phone, then turned to her.

"The phone is on the move, headed north. Agents are triangulating the signal and will intercept the bus."

"We just wait then?" Charlotte asked, still scanning the room, hoping to see her son.

"I'm going to check the bathroom, just in case," Preston said. She came out and went to the counter, spoke to the agents for several minutes, then walked back to Charlotte.

"The bus to New Jersey left an hour ago. We've issued an Amber Alert, and the bus driver is being notified via AlertMedia, their communication system, about what's going on. We don't want to do anything that could make Penelope do something drastic, so agents will be waiting when the bus stops in Atlanta. That's where they'll have to transfer to the next bus."

"Can they stop right now and get him?"

Agent Preston shakes her head. "Penelope will have the bus's itinerary. She knows we're looking for her. If the bus makes an unscheduled stop, who knows what she might do. We have no idea if she has a weapon. If she believes that you are a danger to your son, she could hurt him to keep you from taking him. I know this is torture, but the best plan is to have undercover agents waiting in Atlanta, which will be in another five or so hours."

"What are we waiting for? Let's go!"

"Charlotte, listen to me. We're so close. You've done the opposite of what I've asked at every turn. The last thing we need is for you to be there and for Penelope to see you. You've got to trust me on this."

"Can we drive to Atlanta and park a few miles away? That way when they get him, they can call you and we can get there quickly. He'll be scared. He's already going to be so traumatized."

She nodded. "We can do that. Have you called your husband yet?"

"No."

Agent Preston gave her a strange look. "Why not?"

"He doesn't know I'm here. He told me I was chasing ghosts, so I pretended to be on a business trip. I'll call him when we have Sebastion back."

Agent Preston cast a sidelong look at her while driving. "Charlotte. Is there a reason you don't want your husband to know that we've found him? Do you think he had something to do with this?"

She exhaled a pent-up breath. "Of course not! But he was dead set against my looking into this. I was tired of arguing with him."

"Why is that? That doesn't make sense to me."

Charlotte sighed. "He kept talking about having to pay back the insurance money if the insurance company thought there was a chance Sebastion was still alive." She hesitated, thinking of something else. "When I looked up the phone records, Penelope's call to his phone lasted eleven seconds. He brushed me off when I asked him about that."

The agent was quiet. "You should have told me. We could have discreetly looked into him, and we will now."

Charlotte started to blame herself again. Had she put Sebastion in further jeopardy by keeping her suspicions to herself?

CHAPTER
TWENTY-SEVEN

I pull the blanket up to Sebastion's chin. He fell asleep after only half an hour. I watch him as he sleeps, thinking again what a beautiful child he is. An image of Charlotte flashes through my mind, unbidden. He looks like her; they have the same beautiful cerulean eyes, ivory skin, and delicate features. It irks me that he resembles Charlotte and not me. I know—I'll dye my dark hair blond. I could even get blue contact lenses. Then people will look at him and tell me how much he looks like me.

There's a woman in the aisle across from us with her shoes off, and I wrinkle my nose. I lean over and give her a dirty look.

"It's unsanitary to remove your shoes. Please put them back on."

She returns my dirty look and then scoffs. "Mind your own business, lady."

"Do you want me to tell the driver?" I ask, although I'm not sure I should call attention to us, but hopefully, the threat will be enough.

"Go ahead. Freak."

I tighten my hands into fists, frustrated. "I will at the next stop," I say, needing to have the last word.

"Whatever," she says.

"Jerk," I mutter, but not loud enough for her to hear me. Why can't people just follow the rules? It would make life so much better. Selfish, stupid people ruin everything. I take a deep breath and turn toward the window, watching the miles roll by, feeling lighter with every mile we put between us and Florida. My eyes feel heavy, and I close them, allowing myself to drift off. The next thing I know, I'm being poked in the ribs.

"What?" I snap, my eyes flying open.

"My tummy hurts," Sebastion says.

I reach in my bag and pull out a bag of chips. "Here," I say, handing it to him. "You're probably just hungry."

He shakes his head and puts his hands on his stomach. "No, it hurts."

I really don't need this right now. I sigh and force a neutral tone. Why must he be so difficult? "Sebastion, this is no time for your shenanigans. I know this has been stressful, but everything's going to be fine. I just need you to settle down and try to rest."

"I'm not tired. I wanna go home!" His voice rises, and other passengers look our way.

I reach into my bag and pull out a bottle of chewable Benadryl. "Keep your voice down," I say. "Here, this will make your tummy feel better." I hand him a dose and a half. Hopefully it will knock him out, and I can get some peace.

He takes them from my hand and puts them in his mouth.

"Good, now try to close your eyes and get some sleep, and when you wake up, we'll be that much closer to California."

He quiets down and I look out the window, pondering this latest turn of events. I should probably dye his hair black, like mine. Or maybe I should make us both redheads—then we'll definitely look more alike. I've been researching the nomadic lifestyle. At first, I thought it was only weirdos living that way, but I'm learning that many people find it a liberating way to live. It would certainly help us to stay hidden, and it would be educational for Sebastion to travel the country. It could give us a sense of community without the worry of someone getting too nosy. Those folks know how to mind their own business. And my money would definitely last longer that way. The more I think about it, the more sense it makes. I sigh contentedly, glancing over at Sebastion, who's now knocked out, although moaning a bit in his sleep. I close my eyes and drift off again, dreaming of our new life on the road.

It's dark when I open my eyes again. Sebastion is crying. What now?

"What's wrong, Sebastion?" I say, unable to keep the irritation from my voice.

"My tummy hurts!" He doubles over and I notice that his face is white. Before I can say another word, he vomits all over me. I jump up, disgusted.

The lady across the aisle makes a face. "Eww, your kid's sick."

I give her a dirty look and pick him up, hurrying to the back of the bus and the bathroom. As soon as we're in the cramped area, he starts to get sick again. I turn him in front of the commode. "Do it there," I yell as I wet some paper towels and try to clean my shirt.

When he finishes, I take him back to our seat. "I'll be right back, honey." I approach the driver.

"My son is sick. How long until the next stop?"

"We're twenty minutes from Atlanta. Do you need to call 911 or can he hold off until then?"

"That's fine, thank you."

I figure we'll have to get a room for the night and catch another bus tomorrow. When I get back to my seat, Sebastion is crying and I get withering looks from everyone around us.

"Haven't you ever seen a sick child, before? Mind your damn business!" I scream.

I put a hand on his head. He's warm. He must be getting the flu. We'll have to lie low for a few days, but he'll be okay. "Sweetie, we're stopping soon, and we'll go to a motel where you can lie down."

I do my best to soothe him for the remainder of the ride, and finally the bus comes to a stop. I grab our bags and hurry him off the bus, looking around for a taxi. I notice the woman whose bag I put my phone in. She's being questioned by a police officer. My blood runs cold when I see three more officers standing at the doors to the bus, checking the ID of everyone who gets off. I didn't realize the bus to New Jersey would be making the same stop as our bus.

Shit! I pick Sebastion up and, as discreetly as possible, turn around and walk the other way. Once we're no longer in their line of sight, I run as fast as I can, jostling Sebastion in my arms. I stop when I see a cab and hail it. Only when we're safely inside and driving away do I exhale.

CHAPTER
TWENTY-EIGHT

Agent Preston's phone rang and Charlotte held her breath.

"Yes, okay. You're sure? All right."

She turned to Charlotte with a bleak look.

"They weren't on the bus."

"What? How is that possible? I thought they were tracking her phone."

"They were. She put it in someone's bag. She must have known we were on to her. We can only assume she took another bus, or maybe she left the station. Unfortunately, we have no way of tracking her."

Charlotte's heart sank. "You were right. It's all my fault. If I hadn't interfered—"

Agent Preston put a hand on her. "No, stop. If it weren't for you, we wouldn't even know Sebastion was alive. I know I was tough on you, but this isn't your fault. Everyone found out the truth when I went to talk to them anyhow. It was most likely her sister."

"So, what do we do now?"

"As I said, there's an Amber Alert. We'll also send agents back to her sister's to see if we can monitor her phone. We're going to do everything we can to find him."

Charlotte didn't miss the look of defeat in Agent Preston's eyes. "But there's no guarantee, is there? In fact, it's very likely I'm never going to see my son again, isn't it? I need to call Eli and tell him what's happened."

"Yes, and you should go home. But I don't want you to give up. Penelope's going to mess up, and when she does, we're going to find Sebastion."

But Charlotte knew in her heart that those were just empty words. They had lost the element of surprise. Penelope was smart and determined. It was going to take a lot more than luck to find her.

CHAPTER
TWENTY-NINE

I've been up all night with Sebastion, and he's not getting any better. His fever hasn't broken, and now his stomach is distended. I looked up the symptoms for appendicitis, and he has some of them. I don't know what to do. If it is appendicitis, he'll need treatment, but then we'll be exposed. If I don't take him to the hospital, and it is appendicitis, he could die. On the other hand, if it's just the flu, then I could risk our getting caught for nothing. I never knew motherhood could be so hard. All these decisions and no way to know what the right one is!

I decide to give it a little longer. When I looked it up, it said that complications don't usually occur until after forty-eight hours. So, we still have a little time. And besides, it's probably not even that. I always have had a tendency to jump to the worst conclusion. This is either a twenty-four-hour flu, or just a stomachache from being on the road and him not going to the bathroom. He's probably just constipated.

We're in a fleabag motel off the highway, but they didn't ask for any ID when I slapped some cash on the counter. Sebastion is curled up on the bed, crying, and I'm pacing the floor, wishing he would just be quiet so I can think.

"Any better?" I ask, leaning down to put a hand on his head.

He shakes his head. "It hurts, Mommy!"

"Maybe it's gas. Let's see if you can go to the bathroom." Now that I think of it, I can't remember the last time he had a bowel movement. I pick him up and carry him to the bathroom and seat him on the toilet. He doubles over again, his little arms wrapped around himself.

"I can't," he says, tears running down his face.

"Just try for a few minutes, you might feel better."

He shakes his head pathetically. Why can't he just try harder? This could totally be just gas.

"Just sit there until you go. Then you'll feel better. I promise." Maybe I should give him a laxative. I saw a drugstore around the corner. If he doesn't go in the next hour, I'll run out and get him one.

CHAPTER
THIRTY

Charlotte sat at the airport, waiting for her flight to board. She'd called Eli and told him everything. Eli had been stunned to learn the truth. "My God! I'm sorry for not believing you. He's really alive! That's wonderful!"

"Yes, it is, but I don't know if we'll ever find him." She choked back a sob.

"We will move heaven and earth, Char. We're going to get him back! I can't believe Penelope's had him all this time."

"I know, it's beyond words. I have no idea where she's taken him. What if we never get him back?" Her voice caught and she took a deep breath to keep herself from crying again.

"We will never stop looking. I promise." She could hear the steely determination in his voice.

The announcement for her flight came over the loudspeaker. "I'm boarding. We'll talk more when I get home."

"Love you," he said.

"Love you too."

She stood up and gathered her things but froze when she saw Agent Preston's number flash across her phone screen.

"Has something happened?" she said without preamble.

"We found him! He's at Grady Memorial Hospital."

Her heart beat faster. "Is he okay? What happened?"

"He was brought in by ambulance. Appendicitis. Apparently, it was pretty advanced and it ruptured. He's in surgery now. A nurse recognized his face from the Amber Alert and called the FBI."

"Oh my God! Okay, I'll meet you there."

CHAPTER
THIRTY-ONE

I had to do what any good mother would and put my own safety at risk for the good of my child. I rode with him in the ambulance, declining to give any identification, claiming it had been lost on our bus trip. The paramedics didn't have time to argue with me, because poor Sebastion was in agony by then. I waited as long as I possibly could, but when his screams were so loud that they drew the attention of the manager at the motel, I knew it was time to take him. They said if I'd waited any longer, he might not have made it. So I did a good thing by finally calling. I had him admitted under a fake name, and told them I could pay cash, that we don't have insurance and that my ID was lost. They seemed to believe me. Now I just have to wait this out, and then we'll be on our way again.

As I pace in the waiting room, scenes from the past year flood my mind. Now that he's finally accepted me as his true mother, I can't lose him. I've put in so much work, suffered through all his tantrums and demands, his defiance and his complaining. It can't all be for nothing. He has to make it through the surgery. If he dies, it will be her fault for finding us and making us go on the run. Selfish. That's what Charlotte is. Only caring about her own needs and not allowing Sebastion to thrive in his new life.

I look up as the doors swing open and the doctor walks toward me. I try to read the expression on his face. He looks angry.

"He's out of surgery." He shakes his head. "I don't understand why you waited so long to bring him in. He developed peritonitis, which is life-threatening. Fortunately, we were able to clean the abdominal cavity. Now we have to monitor him for infection."

How dare he lecture me? "I thought he had the flu. We don't have insurance and you doctors and hospitals charge exorbitant fees. Maybe if you didn't, I would have brought him sooner. But I didn't want a ten-thousand-dollar bill for the flu."

His jaw tightens. "He's headed to recovery now."

"When can I see him?"

"A nurse will be out to take you back as soon as he's awake."

"Fine." I won't thank him for doing his job, especially after the way he's just spoken to me. He shakes his head and walks off without another word.

I turn as I hear the elevator ding and see a woman and a man step out. Something about the way they look at me makes my hair stand on end. I'm about to get up and go to the cafeteria when the woman walks up to me.

"Hello, Penelope."

I spring up, my heart beating faster. How does she know my name? "You must have me confused with someone else." I start to walk away but she clamps a firm hand around my arm.

"Get off of me! What do you think you're doing?"

I hear the click of metal and realize I'm being handcuffed. The woman speaks.

"Penelope Watson, you're under arrest for kidnapping. You have the right to remain silent—"

Blood rushes in my ears as she continues reading my rights. "Stop. I have to see my son. He needs me! You can't take me, he's in surgery and—"

They drag me away before I can finish the sentence, and my heart breaks as the image of my son waking up and looking for me flashes in my mind.

CHAPTER
THIRTY-TWO

Agent Preston was waiting for her in the lobby when she got to the hospital. Charlotte ran toward her.

"How is he?"

"Out of surgery and just moved to a room. We arrested Penelope. Another agent has taken her for processing. I wanted to be here for you."

Charlotte was filled with a sense of euphoria and relief. He was safe. Her child was alive and safe! Tears of joy fell from her eyes, and she started to weep, all the pent-up fear and anxiety spilling from her in hitching sobs.

As they rode up in the elevator, she felt as though she would burst. She couldn't believe they had found him. She was finally going to see her son! To hold him in her arms again. To bring him home. They stopped at the nurses' station and were directed to his room. Agent Preston hung back as Charlotte walked toward it. She felt like she was moving in slow motion, everything surreal. Then she saw him. He looked so small and frail lying there.

She ran to him, and he looked up at her. Confusion in his eyes, he started to blink. Charlotte couldn't contain herself. She leaned down and hugged him to her.

"My darling. My darling. I've missed you so much."

He stiffened in her arms. "You didn't want me."

She pulled back. "Is that what she told you?"

"You gave me away."

She shook her head. "No, no. Honey, she lied. She took you away. I've been looking for you. I've been so sad without you." She had no idea if he even knew about the school bus accident, and she didn't want to scare him by telling him she thought he was dead.

He looked at her with skepticism.

"Sebastion, Mommy would never, ever give you away. I'm so sorry that she took you. I love you with all my heart."

This was killing her. The reunion she'd imagined, him happy to see her, the two of them clinging to each other, was a fantasy. Of course he'd be confused. God only knew what other lies Penelope had told him. It didn't matter now. Her son was alive! And she'd get him help. She'd bring him back to her little by little. "Mommy loves you more than—"

"Than all the stars in the sky," he finished.

Tears ran down her face. "Yes, yes." He remembered.

"Mommy, can we go home now?"

"Yes, my love. We can go home."

CHAPTER
THIRTY-THREE

Sebastion was quiet as they pulled into the driveway. He had been in the hospital for four days, and during that time, Charlotte had stayed with him, telling him stories of his life before Penelope and showing him pictures of their family life. He was exhausted and weak from the surgery, so their conversations were sporadic, and she spent most of that time just watching him, reveling in his presence and being grateful for his return to her. Her therapist, Dr. Morrison, was brought up to speed on everything, and despite Eli's desire to fly to Atlanta to be with Sebastion, advised them to wait and let Charlotte and Sebastion have time to bond again so he wouldn't feel overwhelmed. Now they were home, and Charlotte looked at her son nervously, unable to tell what he was feeling.

"Are you ready to go in, honey?"

He nodded, biting his lip.

"Daddy and Harper can't wait to see you."

He didn't answer as they got out of the car. She held out her hand and he took it, grasping it tightly.

"It's okay to be scared. But it's all going to be okay."

When they opened the door, she saw that the living room was filled with balloons and signs that said "Welcome home."

Sebastion looked around in wonder. Eli and Harper walked over to him tentatively. Charlotte could see the tears in both of their eyes and could feel their eagerness, but they held themselves back as the therapist had advised.

Sebastion looked back and forth between the two of them, a slow smile spreading across his face. Eli crouched down and opened his arms. "Hi, buddy. I am so happy to see you."

Sebastion took a small step toward him and then Eli closed the distance and hugged his son, tears falling down his cheeks and his shoulders shaking in sobs. Harper ran over and hugged Sebastion from behind, crying as well.

Sebastion patted Eli's shoulder and spoke softly. "It's okay, Daddy. Don't cry."

Charlotte joined the trio, wrapping her arms around them, and knew in that moment, that they would survive.

CHAPTER
THIRTY-FOUR

Afterward

Charlotte would never stop wondering, if Eli had only answered his cell phone that day, if everything would have been different. Agent Preston's investigation into him confirmed her instincts about him and Madison had been right. It had come out during the investigation in preparation for Penelope's trial. Those eleven seconds on his cell phone when Madison had answered instead of him. Eli had had to come clean. It was one of the most painful conversations of her marriage.

"I didn't know that Penelope had called me. Madison answered the phone."

"And why the hell was she answering your cell phone?"

He'd hung his head, looking at the floor for a few moments. "Her car wouldn't start. She called me to pick her up. One thing led to another . . ." Eli explained. "It was stupid. She was telling me how lonely she was and how much she looked up to me. Then she kissed me. I don't know why I let it happen. I felt horrible afterward. I was in the shower when my phone rang. She answered but the caller didn't identify herself. She thought it was a spam call because the number wasn't in my phone. It was only that one time. I swear."

She'd looked at him in disgust. "You *let* it happen? You need to take responsibility, otherwise . . . I can't even. This is not the time, but I don't even know who you are anymore."

Over the past few months, she had been working on forgiving Eli as well as forgiving herself for sending Sebastion to school that day. It was going to take a lot of marriage counseling, and she didn't know if she would ever really trust him again, but she had to try. Throwing her marriage away over one mistake was not something she wanted to do. Sebastion's world had already been turned upside down. Charlotte agreed to focus on their son first, and deal with her marriage later.

It had been six months since they got Sebastion back. He was almost his sunny self again, although remnants of the trauma remained. Harper was quieter these days, hovering more than usual, always trying to make sure that he was safe. They were all doing their best to move forward without fear and anxiety. Their family had survived, and Charlotte chose to be grateful and live each day with hope.

Penelope was sentenced to twenty years in prison without the possibility of parole. She'd be forty-eight when she got out. Still young enough to live her life. But at least Sebastion would be twenty-five and no longer in jeopardy from her.

Charlotte had debated visiting Penelope to try to understand how she could have done what she'd done, but, in the end, she realized that nothing Penelope could say could make her understand. Nora had told her all about their abusive background and how it had made Penelope hypervigilant regarding the children in her care. She recalled their conversation.

"I'm not making excuses for what my sister did," Nora had said. "I just didn't realize the extent to which our childhood had left her damaged. Both our parents loved their drink more than us, and our father had a violent temper. Our mother did nothing to protect us. Penelope had this idealized view of the perfect mother. No one could live up to it, really."

"I suppose we're all guilty of that to some extent. Does anyone judge a mother more than another woman? I blamed myself for what

I thought happened that day. But what I did wasn't out of neglect. I believed he wasn't really sick. And I was doing everything in my power to keep the house and bills paid while Eli was out of work," Charlotte said.

Nora had nodded. "Penelope's favorite show was *The Brady Bunch*. As old as that show is, she felt like it was the standard for what a family should be. I think the idea that you can make a new family you weren't born into appealed to her."

Charlotte had shaken her head. "I'm sorry, but I still can't understand how she could do what she did. There were times I contemplated ending things. She put me through the darkest days of my life. I hope she gets the help she needs, but I also want her in prison for as long as possible."

Charlotte's text tone pinged, bringing her back to the present. She looked down to read a message from Eli.

Family movie night?

She smiled and typed back.

Perfect.

They had been through hell and back, but they were lucky. They'd been given a second chance. There was work to be done, and a long road ahead. But for now, her family was once again complete, and for that, Charlotte would never stop being grateful.

ABOUT THE AUTHOR

Liv Constantine is a pseudonym of international and *New York Times*–bestselling author Lynne Constantine. She is the coauthor of *The Last Mrs. Parrish*, a Reese Witherspoon Book Club Pick, and her critically acclaimed books have been praised by the *Washington Post*, *USA Today*, the *Sunday Times*, *People* magazine, and *Good Morning America*, among many others, with more than one and a half million copies sold worldwide. Constantine also writes the Jack Logan series under the pen name L. C. Shaw. She has a master's degree from Johns Hopkins University and sits on the board of International Thriller Writers. Her work has been translated into twenty-nine languages, is available in thirty-four countries, and is in development for both television and film. When she's not writing, you can find her curled up with her Lab and Golden Retriever, reading a good book or binge-watching the latest limited series.